IN THE WAKE OF
THE BAGGER

JACK HARTE

A novel commissioned by Sligo County Council

S

Scotus
Press

For
My Mother, Lollie Harte
and
My Father, John Harte (1911-1996)

Author's Acknowledgements

Sincere thanks to Colm McHugh, Pat Pidgeon, Michael Phillips, Jim White, Vergil Nemchev and all associated with Scotus Press

Thanks to Sligo Co. Council who commisioned the novel, and especially to Mary McDonagh, Public Art Officer, and Joe Lee, Curator of the programme, 'Unravelling Developements'.

I raise my glass also to Carrie, Loretta, Owen, George, Joe, Miriam, Matt, and to the memory of Farnan, to Manus who raked the archive, and to all who see in this book reflections of what was.

Published in Ireland by
Scotus Press
PO Box 9498
Dublin 6

Copyright Jack Harte 2006
The moral right of the author has been asserted.

A catalogue record of this book is available from the British
Library.
ISBN 0 9547194 5X

Set in 10pt. New Century Schoolbook

Cover Art-Work & Design Pat Pidgeon
Layout: Pat Pidgeon & Colm McHugh
Back Cover Photo : C.Conmey

1

D o you remember what it was like to watch a horse and plough opening the soil in a green field at the butt end of the winter? That long narrow field along the Wrack Road that slopes in a gentle curve down towards the sea? The man between the handle shafts is urging the horse with little flicks of words, anxious to have the field lying belly-up to catch the first warmth of the sun on Brigid's Day.

And the white birds from the foreshore, hungry from their winter fast, gather in flocks overhead, descend in scavenging raids on the newly opened soil. The squawk and the squeal of them as they jostle for the richest pickings. More birds arrive as the brown band swells across the green sward, and now they settle on the clay, making it their own, working it over, confident that starvation has been held at bay.

The bagger was a bit like that, wasn't it? You surely have no difficulty remembering what the bagger was like, as it caterpillared out on a Midlands bog, all iron bulk and cautious purpose, brandishing tooth and blade, tearing open the spring bog with its shaft of knife-sharp buckets. Deep goes the shaft to plunge and plunder the oozy peat. And the triumphant buckets raise their prize aloft, higher and higher, then tip it over into the churning maw of the machine. And the excretion, squeezed from the steel intestine, is borne on platters, as a Pharaoh's might, out the length of the long spread-arm, to be dropped on the bank, in row after row.

And we followed in the wake of the bagger, like hungry sea birds. From Kerry and Donegal we flocked, from Clare and Mayo, all the lean counties along the west coast of Ireland. And by summer we were scattered out across the turf-bank in clutches and clusters, picking sustenance from the excretion of the bagger, rejoicing in our victory over want, making the earth our own.

2

The road out of Co. Sligo twisted and turned, mile after mile, as if resisting a painful duty. Then when the boundary was near and resistance seemed futile, it led us up to the very summit of the Curlew Mountains.

At a point on the summit, just before we left the county, from which it was possible to see ahead of us the expanse of the Central Plain, and behind us the mountains, valleys, lakes of Sligo, Father asked the driver, Martin Henry, to halt the lorry.

"I want you to see this," he said to me, opening the door and hopping down from the cab. "This is the future." He waved his hand across the landscape in front of us. It was flat, flat as the surface of the sea on a day of calm. And it stretched like a sea in front of us too, as far as we could peer towards the horizon, not a hump nor a hollow, not a mountain nor valley anywhere.

"And it's nearly all bog," said Father. "The centre of Ireland is nearly all bog. The Bog of Allen they call it, and it runs from here to the doorsteps of Dublin. Isn't it amazing? This is the future, young fellow. We'll get the others to take a look."

I stared at this flat expanse, this future, while Father gave his little talk to Mother and the others who were all peering out through the rungs of the crate.

Mother had insisted on travelling in the back with the rest of the family. Father was the one who knew where we were going, so he had to travel in the front and give directions to the driver who had never ventured outside Co. Sligo before. And when I was offered the seat in the cab between Martin Henry and Father, I was quick to accept. However, as soon as I had heard the sing-song rising from the back of the lorry, I suspected I might have made the wrong choice, and that there might have been more fun back there in the nest we had created with the mattresses and bed-clothes in among the table and chairs, dresser, bed-frames, all the furniture we possessed.

Having surveyed the future, I went around to gaze at the past. Three of my brothers were straining their faces through the rungs at different heights. "Where's Ballyclare, Daddy? Can we see Ballyclare yet?" they were asking.

From behind the lorry stretched a very different landscape. The Bricklieve Mountain hulked with its carbuncles of ancient cairns on its back, its side almost sliced off leaving a valley up in the clouds. Father had called it the Windy Gap when he pointed it out, and it was aptly named. Up there was fought the epic battle of Moytura between the Tuatha de Danann and the Fomorians. Beyond that again the dark caves of Keash were set so deep into the mountain the same Tuatha de Danann could still be lurking inside them.

Sweeping down from the side of Bricklieve the landscape plunged into blue lakes, Lough Arrow, Lough Key. Over Bricklieve and around it I strained to catch a glimpse of the Ox Mountains, that long range that separated Tireragh from the rest of Sligo, from the rest of the world. I couldn't be sure that the one snip of dark blue on the horizon was of my mountain range; it could have belonged to Ben Bulben or Knocknarea. So I focussed on the fluffy clouds close to the horizon and imagined how even at that moment, they were looking down directly on Easkey and Killeenduff and Dromore West. And I stayed looking at them until Father summoned me back to the cab.

As I passed the back of the lorry, Mikey shouted, "Robbie, Frank peed in your wellington."

There was an outburst of laughter from the darkness behind the rungs of the crate.

"Never mind them, Robbie," Mother said. "They made that story up just to tease you."

"No, it's true, Robbie," said Mikey. "He was bursting, and there was no place to do it. We were shouting for Daddy to

stop the lorry, but he didn't hear us. None of ye heard us. So
Frank took up your wellington and peed into it." Again
there was an explosion of amusement deep among the
stacked chairs and the bedsteads.

"Don't heed them, Robbie," again came Mother's voice,
calm and assertive. "Your wellington was caught in that
shower back there and got wet, so they made up the story
about Frank to see if they could annoy you. They're just jealous because you're travelling in the front with Daddy."

Again there were hoots of derisive merriment until
Mother's voice became stern and restored order.

I wracked my mind trying to remember what shower she
was talking about, wondering how the rain could have pen-
etrated the tarpaulin to target my wellington when everything else seemed dry. However, Father was urging me back
into the cab. I decided that I had been too wrapped up in my
own thoughts to be aware of a thunderstorm, not mind a
shower.

And the lorry began to wind down the side of the
Curlews, down to the plain.

Now there was only one thought in my mind, one. Why?
Why exchange our landscape of sea-cliffs and rocky shores,
of mountains and rivers, of grey boulders and rushy fields,
for this flat expanse where one could see nothing beyond the
few mean fields on either side of the road? Why? Why leave
the sheltered barony where we knew everyone, where everyone knew us, where we were related to every thing that
moved? Why? Why?

I listened to Father elaborating to Martin Henry the case
for the move. There would be work, jobs with wages at the
end of the week, schools and colleges to educate the children. It was his theme for the past while, every time he
returned to Killeenduff. He had left abruptly the previous
summer, walked out of the forge, closed the door, and left,
just like that. The doors had remained closed with the coal
dust and ashes resting on the anvil and the bellows, the
bars of fresh iron pitched along the wall.

He returned regularly at weekends to tend the crops and

save the turf. And gradually he began to talk of a new life, for all of us, in the Midlands, where this immense project was afoot to put the bogs of Ireland to commercial use. There were machines as big as houses, bigger than some of the houses we knew, and teams of men, by the dozen, by the hundred, in the summer even by the thousand, all attacking the bogs of Ireland, and harvesting stacks of turf so long the eye could not follow nor the mind weigh.

Father had gone to Ballyclare where a Tireragh man, Willie Morahan, was the foreman in charge of one of the biggest bogs in the Midlands. Willie gave him a job on the spot. However, as he was in charge of outside operations he could employ only labourers. The workshops were the domain of a rival foreman. But between the workshop and the open bog there was a forge. Here Father was installed, employed as a labourer, but doing smith work, tradesman's work. Willie assured him it would be a temporary arrangement only, that he would get full recognition as a tradesman and full wages before long.

For six months Father had lived in a hostel, or in the 'billets' as he sometimes called it. Occasionally when he came back for weekends he would talk a little of the hostel, the way he lived there, and the men from all quarters who were billeted with him. It was strange, so strange. There were rows and rows of huts with hundreds of men crammed into them, sleeping in bunks, cooking for themselves, sometimes playing cards or football in the evenings after work, after eating, sometimes just sitting around the stove talking.

And now here we were, the whole family, lock, stock, and barrel, all loaded on to Martin Henry's lorry, careering towards the future that Father talked about so optimistically.

When we were approaching the village of Ballyclare, Father asked Martin to slow down.

"Now, we are going to leave the province of Connaught. And wait until you see this river."

We came to a bridge and again his sweeping hand urged us to take in the view. I noticed that Martin was keeping his

16

eyes riveted to the narrow bridge, his fists tightened around the steering wheel. But I looked left and right over the parapets, and I was impressed. The river must have been a hundred yards wide under the bridge, then downstream pushed its banks at least a mile apart before flowing off into a lake in the distance. Yes, I was impressed. My experience of rivers had never extended beyond ones I could cross on foot without getting my knees wet.

Slowly we drove up the dozy little village which looked like any of the dozy little villages we had passed through on the way from Sligo. But at the top of the village, opposite the chapel, we swung around to the right, and there I saw something different, something I had not seen before, rows of newly built houses, all alike.

"This is it," said Father. "This is where we're going to live."

So this was The Park that we had been hearing about for months, that we had been trying to imagine.

"I had my choice of any house but two," Father was explaining to Martin Henry. "Only two were taken before me. I could have taken the round house there." He pointed at an absolutely quaint-looking house, totally round but for a square block stuck on. I fancied that house immediately. It looked like one from the illustrations in fairytale books.

"And why didn't you?" I asked.

"No garden worth talking about. I picked the one with the biggest garden, so we can plant enough vegetables to keep us going."

We drove up through the estate past the rows of two-storey houses, then turned left into the rows of one-storey houses.

"Here we are," he said, pointing, "the very first one, No. 33, The Park. What do you think of it?" He directed the question at me while Martin swung the lorry into a lane beside it.

"It looks great," I said. "And there's a shed."

"Yeah, that will keep the turf dry for the winter."

We got out. Father and Martin went to the back of the

17

lorry to release the rest of them.

"So this is it, Daddy? Are we here?" Eileen's voice and Mikey's voice brimmed with excitement.

They stripped back the tarpaulin, took off the back crate, and lowered the tail-board. Out tumbled my brothers, my sister, and finally Mother stepped down gingerly, supported on either side by the upreaching hands of Father and Martin Henry.

Father led the way into the house. We followed tremulously. He clearly enjoyed parading his privileged knowledge, strutting through the house as if he had built it himself. "This is the kitchen, with the range. Out the back here is the scullery with the sink, and the water coming from the taps, hot and cold."

We had never seen water flowing from taps before, not to mind hot water. We had never seen a flush toilet before, and my brothers pulled the lever again and again, just to watch that miniature waterfall in total fascination. And the corridor, with the doors leading off it, was like a maze after our three-roomed cottage in Tireragh, where you could go from the kitchen to the upper room or to the lower room, nowhere else. Here there were three bedrooms, and a bathroom, as well as the scullery and the kitchen. My sister and brothers had already begun to play hide-and-seek when Father called on me to help carry in the furniture.

We set up the big double bed and a single bed in the front bedroom, two single beds in one of the back bedrooms, and one single in the other.

"Who's going to sleep here?" shouted Mikey. "Where are we going to sleep?"

"This will be the boys' room," declared Mother, standing in the space between the two single beds in the back room. "Mikey and Cormac will sleep in this bed, Frank and Billy in this one."

"Where will Robbie sleep?" asked Mikey suspiciously.

"He will sleep in the single bed in the front room."

"That's not fair, why does Robbie get a bed all to himself?"

"Because he's the biggest. Would you like to share your

bed with him?"

"And have him bossing me and kicking me – no I would n't."

"Well then?"

"And does that mean that Eileen will have a room all on her own?" Mikey was trying to work out the logic of it all.

"Yes, but when we save some money we will buy another bed for that room in case anyone comes to visit."

"But we all slept in the one room at home."

"This is our home now, and we have more rooms, so we can divide up."

When Mother turned to oversee the unpacking of the delft and the pots in the scullery, Mikey stuck his tongue out at me, and began to bounce up and down on the bed to test its springs.

3

You are inside me like the effigy at the core of a Russian Doll. Do you know what a Russian Doll is? Of course not. It was a cowboy's cap-gun you got from Santa, Christmas after Christmas, the greatest toy of all. Up in Dowdican's field with the boys, shooting and killing, dying and living, among the crags and the bushes and those dangerous little stretches of open terrain where you could be mown down by the badmen, where later the brightest primroses would bloom. And when your supply of caps was spent, you would improvise, 'bang, bang', and when the gun fell apart you would fashion a crude imitation from a forked branch of an ash tree, and carry on, undeterred.

Well, a Russian Doll is a doll within a doll, within a doll. You are at the core. Inside me. A little smiling manikin. You do not grow, you do not change. You have merely added skin upon skin, like welts, each new mask a defiant reproduction of the first. It is as if some original pain aches at the centre and throws up all these epidermal shields to ward off greater affliction from without. Is it thus with everyone, with everything? Does even the giant oak nurse some primordial wound that it sprouts a new bark against the onslaught of each new winter? I don't know.

Could you not have changed, evolved? Could each new coat not have been more than a disguise? Could each new face not have been the licence to pursue a new life free of all your pain and principles? Why must you remain inside me with all your hurt and all your ecstasy? Why must I be crusted on the outside, stratified, a hollow shell, whose obligation seems to be to cradle the soft kernel where pain and joy were possible, where both were still natural. It seems that it is I, not you, that is the effigy.

And what must I do to reach you? Break shell after shell? Peel off the welted coats you donned against the icy winds of living? Or pierce straight to the core with a single well-directed shaft?

4

The Horse Fair in Ballyclare fell during the first week of February. It was a local holiday. Schools closed and everyone downed tools to celebrate the Horse Fair. Even the Turf Company had given the men the day off. In early February there wasn't much work for them anyway.

"It used to be a big one," said Father. "One of the biggest. As big as Ballinasloe. But the horses have had their day. We'll have a look around anyway. We might do a bit of business." He held Frank by the hand and Mikey and I followed them down the concrete footpath.

When we turned the corner we saw the crowds on the green in front of the chapel, lorries with their dung-splattered tail-boards sloped to the ground, horses frisking about. It was certainly the biggest fair I had ever seen, and it was all horses they were selling, no cattle, no sheep. When we reached the chapel we were able to look down the main street and across the bridge to the Connaught side. Everywhere was packed with horses and people and hawkers' stalls.

"A man would get plenty of shoeing to do here," joked Father, referring to his trade.

"Why don't you tell them you're a blacksmith?" I prompted.

He looked at me sharply. "I have finished working for the poor old farmers. Do you know how hard it is to get money out of a farmer? You shoe a horse for him or mend his plough and he says he will pay you as soon as he sells the potatoes or the surplus hay. Then you are anxious about the weather all summer and watching the stalks rising from his drills, hoping the blight won't attack them before the spuds are seasoned. What kind of a way is that to earn a living?"

"You could make him pay when you do the job."

"And if he says he hasn't the money yet – what then? How do you know if he is really short, or if he is just trying to put off paying you? And if he is short, how can you turn him away?"

"Was that why you gave up the forge?"

"It wasn't the poor farmers that annoyed me, it was the rich ones. Do you know that a man came to me one time, a man who had plenty of land and plenty of money, a man who was a hell of a lot better-off than I was. He wanted a job done, and I said I would do it for him. But I didn't have the right steel. I gave him the specification and told him to go and pick it up, and that when he brought it back I would do the job for him. Do you know what he said to me? He asked if he would charge it to my account, or would I give him the money to buy the steel? Now, how do you work for people like that without letting it break your heart?"

I had no answer. Was that what it took to uproot us from Tireragh? Was that why he had pulled the door of the forge behind him and left the lengths of bright steel to rust and flake into the earth floor?

"Still, we might do some useful business here," he said after an interval, as if he wanted to participate in this melee of festivity. And we walked on with a lighter step.

Mikey and Frank were open-mouthed staring at all the horses, at the haggling owners and buyers, and the hawkers at their stalls selling everything from tools to clothes to shoe-polish. The shop-fronts were barricaded with planks on porter-barrels so that the animals would not go through the plate-glass windows.

At the bottom of the hill, in the centre of the village, was a crossroads, and on the corner stood a grocery shop-with-pub called the Eagle. As we neared the front door we could hear the sound of a flute playing a traditional tune.

"That sounds good," said Father. "He can play."

We edged in to the front of the shop, where they sold the groceries. It was packed with men sitting on stools drinking porter, obviously an overflow from the bar which was further inside and separated from the shop by the merest suggestion of a partition.

The flute player was just inside the front door. We stood there listening to him until he had finished the tune. There was a cheer as he took the flute from his lips. "Good man, the Shan. More power to you."

"That was a tidy bit of playing," said Father to him when the clamour had abated.

"And where are you from, my good man?"

"I'm from Sligo," said Father, "where we know a good tune when we hear one."

"If you come from Sligo, you would surely. There's plenty of music down that part of the country."

"There might be plenty of music, but you can't feed the mouths of children with music. That's why we're here."

The old man glanced at Father and then glanced at us with a sharp eye from under the rim of his hat. "You must have come to live in The Park."

"We have indeed."

"Then you're welcome to Ballyclare, and may you be content here."

"Thanks. I know we will. The old flute is serving you well," said Father nodding at the severely weathered instrument.

"Ach, it's not playing as well as it should be," he declared, lifting it and examining it as if consideration of its condition was not something that weighed too heavily on him. "It's a while since I played it. It needs to be kept oiled like the rest of us, or it won't perform." He took a mouthful of porter from his glass and spat it into the mouth-hole. Then he rolled the barrel of the flute in his hands, trying to rinse the inside round about with the porter. Then he shook the dregs from the flute down on to the floor, while the three of us children took an involuntary step backwards to avoid the splatter. "That should improve it." He nodded at Father. "This one is for you."

He started playing a lively tune, and whether it was my imagination playing tricks on me or not, I thought the flute sounded the better for its oiling.

24

"The Boys of Ballisodare – that's the tune he's playing," whispered Father, chuffed that the musician had honoured him with a Sligo tune.

When the flute had fallen silent again, Father asked the player. "Do you know any farmer who would have a rood or two to let as conacre? I want to plant some spuds and vegetables as soon as there's a stir in the ground."

The old man again cast that quick glance at Father from under the rim of his hat. "Did someone send you to me?"

"No, why?"

"I thought you might have heard I had a bit of land to let."

"No," said Father. "You're the first person I asked."

"Then you hit on the right man."

"That's mighty. You have a couple of roods to spare then?"

"As much as you want."

"Two roods will be plenty."

"I'll show you the field and let you mark it out yourself."

"What about rent? How much is conacre around here?"

"Ach, I won't be too hard on you."

"Still, I'd like to strike a bargain."

"What will you be setting?"

"Spuds, cabbage, vegetables."

"Would it suit you to throw me a few bags of spuds?"

"Instead of rent? That would suit me very well."

"Then we'll leave it at that."

"Grand."

"Come out tomorrow and I'll show you the ground."

"Where will I find you?"

"Go out the Ballymahon road for about a mile."

"It will be some evening, next week. And what's the name?"

The old man shot him that glance again, as if it was a personal question.

"So that I can find you," explained Father.

"You'll have no bother finding me. Ask anyone for the Shan's house."

"That's grand," said Father. "And my name is Joe Dowd." The Shan kept looking at Father dubiously, as if he had never before encountered this ritual of exchanging names and viewed it with suspicion. But Father nodded all around to the other men as we withdrew from the pub.

Outside, back among the horses, and the rising bed of dung, and the din of excited talk, Father threw back his head and laughed. "I never thought I'd see the day when a farmer would be waiting for my crops to grow."

5

D o you remember a day in Killeenduff when Mother promised to take you all to the sea? It was summer and the sun was shining. But she was busy with the usual chores, and you were helping, reluctantly, and Eileen and Mikey were helping and grumbling. Eventually the chores were complete, the togs and towels packed, the rug rolled up tight under Mother's arm. And you set off merrily down the Wrack Road.

But when you arrived at the Cimin and looked over at the sweep of Cuanmore bay, you found that the tide had gone out. You were too late. The bay was no longer full, the water was not lapping the shingle as it was whenever you came to bathe. And you looked at the exposed rocks with dismay.

Mother was probably disappointed too, disappointed that the responsibility of the day's duties had caused her to miss the tide. But she told you to make the most of it, to tog out and bathe in the rock pools the tide had left behind. And you did that. You went from one pool to another trying to find enough water, trying to re-create from the cupfuls that were left behind the fullness of the open sea. Do you remember?

It is like that now with me. I have come back. I have come back to keep your promise. But the tide is gone. I wanted to catch the tide, imagined the bay would be always full, but I delayed too long over my chores, my obligations, my responsibilities

The same tide will never flood the bay again. And I am going from pool to pool, the meagre remnants of the life I knew, trying to recreate it in all its fullness. And the unspeaking ghosts hover about me with accusing looks.

Why do you smile at my desperation, you who made the promise? Don't you see it is my own need I serve now? I want to crack these shells, toss them aside, and find again the soft kernel where pain and joy were possible, where love was inhaled like the salt air, and beauty never failed to stir the blood.

6

In March the baggers moved out on the bog. "They were a sight to see," declared Father as he peeled his spuds, with a hint of pride, a suggestion of a job complete, as if he were personally responsible for sending them forth in such fettle.

"When can we see one, Daddy?" shouted Mikey from the bottom of the table, his enthusiasm divided between eating his dinner and listening to Father.

"Soon," said Father, as though he were ruminating over every rivet he had driven into the machines to get them ready for the cutting season. Every evening over dinner we had been given a briefing on how the work was progressing and fretted over every problem and every setback, as if we too had a personal stake in these machines. "Soon," he repeated.

"But when, Daddy, when?" Mikey was not to be put off by a vague answer.

"On Sunday, if it's not raining, I'll bring one of you down on the bike?"

"Can I go, Daddy? Can I go?" Mikey stopped mashing his potato into his cabbage soup and sat upright with his fork brandished skywards in his fist, like a warrior holding a spear.

"Well, I think it should be the eldest first," interjected Mother. "And each one will have a turn."

"But that means Robbie will get first, and he always gets first," protested Mikey.

"That's the way it is. If you were the eldest, you would get first," insisted Mother.

Mikey turned his fork around and stabbed his spuds with passion. "It's not fair," he said.

"There has to be a system," said Mother. "If the system is

that the eldest goes first, and it is implemented, then it is fair."

"Alright," said Mikey, fork at ease again, "what about the baths on Saturday night? How come Robbie doesn't have to go first then? Oh, no, it's the youngest goes first then, and Robbie gets to stay up latest."

"How would you like to go last then," interjected Eileen, "and use the water after everyone else?"

"Use the water after you and Robbie? No thanks."

"Well, we have to use it after you've been in it, and Frank, and Billy, and Cormac. So, what are you moaning about?"

They were referring to the ritual on Saturday night when the whole family had to have a turn in the bath. The range was not very effective at heating the water in the pipes, so we had to boil additional water in kettles and saucepans. Then, one after another, we got in and scrubbed the week's dirt off. By the time Mother and Father had washed themselves, the water was not attractive. However, we were still commenting on the improvement over the old galvanised bath we used to place in the middle of the kitchen floor back in Killeenduff.

"I'm not saying I want to be always first or last. It's just that Robbie always seems to get the best deal," Mikey's fork, no longer a weapon, was stirring the mashed potato into a whipped cream.

"That's because you are never satisfied with what you have yourself. You had a nice hot dinner in front of you and now you've let it go cold while you were arguing about nothing." Mother's tone was emphatic.

Mikey looked at his dinner, put down the fork, took up a big spoon, and began to ladle the liquefied potatoes into his pout.

Father had a big Rudge bicycle. I chose to ride on the carrier rather than be cramped and crouched in front of him on the handlebars. He had to turn his head to talk to me, and had to raise his voice to counter the strong wind that was blowing from the left side.

"Willie Morahan might be down here," he said.

"On a Sunday?" I shouted back and moved my backside on the carrier to re-distribute the discomfort.

"That's Willie. Even on a Sunday."

I was excited. I was excited at the prospect of seeing a bagger after hearing so much about it. I was now also excited by the expectation of meeting Willie Morahan, a man from Tireragh who was leading the drive to turn the bogs of Ireland into turf. I was hoping that we might start a conversation about home, places we knew, people of mutual acquaintance.

We cycled about two or three miles, then came to a level crossing where a railway line intersected the road. Father halted and I hopped off stiffly. He propped the bike against a clump of furze and we took to the rail track. The Company transported the turf along this line down to a tip-head near the workshop where lorries came from Dublin to be loaded, Father explained. They had locomotives and steel wagons plying up and down the bog all the time.

We walked along the line for about a mile, passing what Father called virgin bog on either side: it had never been cut. Then we came upon the first of the trenches. It took my breath away. Like a huge drain, twenty yards wide, it stretched off into the distance on either side of the railway line and at right angles to it. Sloping up from the edges of the trench on either side were two smooth banks, each over fifty yards wide, and at the top of the banks were two clamps of saved turf. The straight lines of the clamps and the banks and the trench stretched off into the distance. I marvelled at the enormity of this landscape created by the hand and the industry of human beings.

"This is Trench One," said Father. "The trench is the wide drain in the centre, but when the Company talk about Trench One, they are talking about the drain, the two banks and the two clamps that go with it. The baggers will be down on Trench Three and Trench Four, at the centre of the bog. Those are the longest open and the best drained. A bagger would sink out there like a stone in water." He pointed at the soggy quality of the turf bank in front of us.

31

All the bogs I had ever seen were soggy, so I found it hard to imagine a bog that was not. We continued along the railway line, which was intersecting the trenches diagonally and probably around the halfway point, as the trenches, banks, and turf-clamps, all seemed to converge at the horizon on either side.

When we reached the third trench, and therefore, according to Father, the centre of the bog, there was indeed a drier more compact feel underfoot. He looked up and down, but there was no sign of activity. However, we could hear from somewhere a din of voices against a rhythmic clanging of mechanical noises. We walked past the clamps towards the fourth trench, and there in front of us loomed a huge hulk of a machine, amber yellow against the dark brown of the bog. My eyes struggled to comprehend the scene in its enormity.

"That's the bagger," said Father simply as we both stood looking perhaps equally in awe.

Sitting right on the very brink of the trench was the enormous machine. It had an arm projecting down into the trench and an equal distance up into the air, at a tilt like the extended instrument of a tipsy melodeon player. On the arm was a belt rotating with buckets fixed crossways so that when they rose up out of the bank they were full of peat. Up the belt the buckets went until they reached the top, then revolved to come down the opposite side, tipping their load into a gaping hole in the body of the machine. Then down again and around relentlessly scooping a margin off the bank.

As we approached, Father was pointing out features, and explaining them in animated detail. I could see that the bagger was squeezing out an endless secretion of masticated peat shaped like two sods of turf but without break. These two limitless lines of wet muck eased on to a conveyor belt which carried them out on a long spread-arm the whole length of the turf bank, a distance I estimated at fifty yards or so. The spread-arm was a fascinating contraption of wheels and levers and belts and pulleys which supported the conveyor belt and moved along the bank in time with the bagger, keeling over as soon as the rows of peat extended to the top of the bank. With simple ingenuity, a row of metal disks following the spread-arm sliced the lines of peat into proper-sized sods, about a foot long.

Despite the ingenuity and the complexity of this mechanical monster, I could see immediately that, apart from whatever motor throbbed at its heart, the lot of it might have been produced in my father's forge.

While my eyes wrestled with the vastness of the machine, my ears strained to analyse the explosion of sounds emanating from this nucleus of activity so at odds with the absolute silence of the infinite bog. The regular throb of the motor was punctuated by the loud shouts of men's voices. And there were men about, dozens of them, chasing hither and thither, shouting to one another and at one another.

When I looked closely I saw that most of them were engaged in relaying huge wooden planks, lifting them from behind the bagger, carrying them forward, and laying them in front of the machine.

"What are they doing?" I asked Father.

"The ground is soft where the bagger is now. At this time of year a lot of it is. The planks keep the bagger from sinking. That's about the toughest job you could ask men to do, planking the bagger at this time of year. - I'm sure they're happy to be out here on a Sunday," he added wryly.

"Did you do any work on this bagger?"

"Do you see those buckets?" he pointed to the rows of buckets on the cutting arm that were slicing up through the turf bank "I welded together every one of those buckets."

I watched with pride the sharp edges knifing through the bog.

"By God, Morahan is here. He's some man. He doesn't have to come out on a Sunday, you know." He nodded in the direction of a man in a white shirt who had emerged into view from the other side of the machine. His incongruous white shirt was open at the neck and the sleeves were rolled up above the elbows. "He's the Production Foreman, and by

God he takes the job seriously."

My heart leaped, leaped with pride at the sight of a Tireragh man in charge, shouting orders, directing people, leaped in anticipation of meeting this Tireragh man and of hearing another Sligo accent for the first time since we crossed the Curlews.

There must have been as many as thirty men hovering around the machine. A couple were in the cab, obviously the drivers. Another couple were keeping surveillance on the spread-arm. The rest were involved in this continuous task of lifting the wooden planks from behind the bagger, carrying them forward, and laying them in the path of the machine.

Father pointed out the huge caterpillar tracks of the machine itself, on which it was creeping forward on this causeway of planks. "Most of the time the caterpillar tracks are enough to keep it afloat, but when the bog is very wet they have to plank it as well. I'll tell you this much, it's a rough job."

I could see that for myself. Some of the men were stripped to the waist as they waded through muck and water, despite the chill wind that kept my overcoat buttoned to the neck. They rooted up each plank that the bagger had pressed down into the bog, heaved it up on their shoulders, carried it as far as the spread-arm and passed it over to their fellow-workers on the other side. They in turn carried the planks shoulder-high to lay them in the path of the lumbering hulk of metal that was going to press them down into the bog once more.

There was something almost feverish about the pace of the work, about the shouts and curses of the men that rose above the dull monotonous rhythm of the motor and the clanking of the moving arms. Willie Morahan was standing over them and his shouts and curses were loudest of all. I recognised his Sligo accent immediately. He swore at the men for not moving fast enough, cursed the bagger, and the planks, and the bog. The men in turn swore at one another, complained about each other. This drew further curses and threats flailing down on their bare backs in the Sligo accent. I was shocked and terrified. I had never before seen adults treat one another like this. There was so much concentrated aggression and hatred, I expected at any moment a brawl to erupt.

We were close enough now to see the men's faces, but their eyes were concentrated and preoccupied, their brows tightened, as they lifted the sodden planks and heaved them across to the men on the other side. They were all sweating from the effort and breathing in snorts like horses straining under a load. Their faces and arms and clothes were smeared with the wet muck. Every step they took as they shouldered the planks required them to pull their feet out of the suck of the wet bog.

Father continued pointing out the various components of the bagger, but it was the sight of so many men heaving and sweating and shouting and swearing that had me transfixed. Not one of them raised his head in recognition or greeting in the usual country way. Daubed with the grime of the bog, it was as if they had donned masks and were compelled to act out some weird scene that they did not enjoy or understand.

Willie Morahan came around to us when he saw Father standing on the bank. I had lost interest in listening to the cadence of his Sligo accent, after hearing his screaming curses in that sacred voice. It was a desecration that had left me frozen, that had chilled me more than the March wind, that had dampened my spirit even more than the sight of so many men gouging huge sodden planks out of the dripping bog. He nodded in my direction and winked when Father pointed me out as his son.

They conversed for quite a while, Morahan breaking off occasionally to scream fresh abuse at someone or other. I rambled off to watch the long unending smudge of macerated peat being squeezed on to the spread-arm in a double row, to watch this smudge being borne relentlessly on the steel plates of the spread-arm out and out to the very end of this conveyor belt, then, at the exact moment it reached the end, to watch the sudden flip as the whole conveyor belt, from the bagger to the extremity near the turf clamp, revolved in a clap and left the two rows of kneaded peat beside each other on the ground. I climbed up on the clamp of dry turf to view the scene behind the bagger. As far as the eye could see there were rows upon rows of the spread peat scored neatly into the size of sods by the phalanx of metal disks following the spread-arm. I took up a dry sod from the clamp underneath me, the remainder of the previous year's harvest. It was difficult to imagine the dollops of sludge in front of me hardening eventually into these rock-like sods. But there they were in the tidy endless clamp waiting their turn to be transported down the railway line to the yard.

Eventually Father whistled to me. He had finished talking to Morahan, and the foreman was walking back to the gang of labourers, announcing his return by a fresh burst of swearing.

"Well, have you seen enough?" asked Father.

"Who are those men?"

"They're all employed full-time by the Company. Did you not recognise any of them? Some of them are from The Park. Johnny Kincaid was there. Did you not recognise Johnny? He's up in Number Forty Two. And so was Billy McCormack from Number Twenty Six down in the two storey houses. Did you not see him there?"

"No, they were all black, and anyway they didn't even look up. Why did they not look up, or say hello?"

Father laughed. "This isn't Sligo you're in now, young fellow. This is what it's like to be working for the Turf Company. They pay you to work, and not to cock your backside on a fence and talk to your neighbour. Oh, no, that day is gone, and no harm either. Men were made to work, not to be blowing hot air."

I was silent a while, not sure that I agreed with him. There was nothing sweeter in the old country than to be walking along the road and have a neighbour stop his work and amble over to the fence just to have a chat with you. Father's passion for work I could not argue against, although he was inclined to bore us children with his long sermons on the virtue of work, with his equally protracted diatribes against those he felt were not earning the air they breathed. And his list included politicians, and priests, and managers everywhere.

We were walking back on the railway line when he spoke again. "Isn't Willie Morahan a mighty man all the same?"

"Why?"

"Would you believe that the engineers didn't want to let out the baggers for another while. They said the bog was too soft. But Willie insisted, he wanted them out to start production. He rounded up all the labourers, every man jack of them, and put them out planking the baggers, around the clock, three shifts a day. And see how much he has cut already. Of course if a bagger sinks, he'll be in big trouble. And he says there's a few who wouldn't mind seeing him slip. Jealous as hell, they are. But there's no danger of Willie slipping up. There he is on a Sunday with his jacket off, driving them on."

"It looks dangerous, what they're doing." I wanted to change the subject as I could not share Father's admiration for Willie Morahan.

"Of course it's dangerous. Last year a man called Paddy Byrne got caught in the macerator. He lost his balance, or maybe slipped. Anyway he was in pulp before they could stop the motor. A nice man he was too, harmless, from over the Connaught side, and he left a wife and three children."

That horrified me even more, and we fell silent again. The sleepers did not permit a rhythmic walk as in places they were pitched close to one another, in other places very widely apart, so that I was either jorking along in chicken steps, or throwing my legs in front of me in goose steps.

Back on the bike again, Father broke from his musing. "I spoke to Willie about my rate. He said he would raise it with the bods and that he would be sure to get it for me."

"Is there still a problem with the rate?"

"It's the same problem - they're paying me only the labourer's rate, even though I'm a qualified tradesman, and doing the work of a qualified tradesman."

"Is there much of a difference?"

"Of course there is. Tradesmen are paid about twenty-five per cent more than labourers."

"And why won't they give it to you?"

"Pure badness and meanness. I spent five years serving my time, slaving for a master blacksmith down in Riverstown, without getting as much as a penny piece. I did all the exams and got all my papers. So I'm just as qualified as any of the fitters or turners. And I'm doing the same work as the rest of them, a hell of a lot more than some. But they're trying to maintain that there's no such category as blacksmith employed by the Company. They're making out that I'm employed as a labourer on the production side, and that they can pay me only as a labourer. It's as if I never spent a day serving my time. But Willie will sort them out yet. I have every confidence in Willie."

That night I woke up time and time again from a vision of men with daubed faces, and daubed arms, and daubed chests, working frantically before the relentless advance of the insatiable bagger. And the curses of Willie Morahan lashing their stooped backs were goading them on. Whenever they slackened or rested, the hungry machine would advance and suck a man into the macerator, mash him to pulp, sending his flesh and blood wheeling out over the long spread-arm, mixed forever with oozing peat. And if Father was a labourer, then he too could be sent down to heave the planks, he too could be sucked into the macerator and flesh and bone and blood disappear into the ooze and fibre of the bog.

7

What urge guided my steering wheel when I took that detour along the coast road? Was it the shock of visiting Anthony that same day the fateful hand of mortality had been laid on his shoulder? Until then I had postponed the dream, thought that time would deliver all things, that possibility would never close its door on me.

Was it the added shock of seeing the gigantic windmills swaggering on the brow of the Ox Mountains, on that very spot where giants stood in the landscape of your child's mind, trying to best each other in boulder-throwing feats? Did I swing the car to follow the trajectory of their throws back towards Killeenduff? Did I want to verify once more that the favourite, the great Fionn, had failed to hit the seashore like his rival? Did I want to ensure that the rock he split in anger still stood in that open field beside the schoolhouse? Giants and power-generating windmills went to battle in my mind, yes, and sent me searching.

And what about the shock of driving into Dromore West, a shining new metropolis spread across the landmarks that you knew so well? The sleepy village that Mother came from, where her ancestors had baked bread for the people of Tireragh back almost to the time of the Famine, is no more. You would scarcely recognise it now. The ball-alley and the old mill are still there. So is the waterfall, and the few cut-stone remnants of the castle in which Red Hugh spent his last Irish Christmas. They are still there. But all around are houses, offices, supermarkets, even suburban-style estates. I strained to recognise. Perhaps it was that that drove me up the coast road in search of old certainties, in search of something that had not succumbed to the mowing machine of grim Time.

How strange then to approach the old house, and find it

still unchanged, still huddled side-by-side with Anthony's, a bit bedraggled, weather-beaten, but still standing, still defiant.

And what a shock, then, to see a dark-suited man in the garden, hammering down his auctioneer's sign, 'For Sale', hammering it into the very earth you played on, the earth that was watered with Father's sweat, the earth that our hens rooted from the butt of the fuchsia bushes.

And I recognised the auctioneer. You knew his father. He bundled you into his horse-cart once and took you off to the bog, showed you the glen that was home only to the plover and the hare, named for you the gaunt trees that were laden with red berries, mountain ash, rowan. And you never forgot those incongruous berries, you yearned for them as Grüinne did in the old story when she thought she would die if she did not feast on the succulent flesh of those perhaps self-same berries.

But the auctioneer is a business man with an office in town. He is surprised, probably intrigued, when I push open the small wrought-iron gate that still bears the marks, through all the rust, of Father's hammer, and say, 'I'll take it'.

8

Jim the Shan was prepared to give us as much conacre as we wanted. His farm had all the appearance of being left fallow anyway, and as we had to repay him with some of the produce, Father decided it would not be an imposition to take a generous two roods.

A local farmer who had a tractor for hire laughed when Father asked him to plough the field. "The Shan's field is it? You'd lose five ploughs in there before you'd be done. It's nothing but roots underneath. I never saw anything like it. They must have had a jungle or a forest growing there in the old days. Your best bet is to get someone who isn't familiar with the temperament of that field."

After petitioning several tractor owners, Father eventually got one to take on the job. He may not have been aware of the field's reputation, or he may have been desperate enough to take the work regardless. Anyway the finished product was a sad spectacle. He scarcely broke the sod on the surface. It was a far cry from the neatly drilled pattern of normal tillage.

"What will we do with it?" I asked Father, as we surveyed the lamentable effort.

"We'll have to cultivate it in the old way," he replied despondently.

"What way is that?"

"In ridges, lazy beds. The way we did it on the side of the mountain, or in rocky gardens back in the West. I thought we were away from all that, but here goes."

He took the shovel and began to scoop a trench down through the field, scattering the excavated soil to left and right. When he had gone a little distance, he stopped and doubled back, scoring a second trench about three feet from the first one. He then went over to the hedgerow, selected a strong ash sapling and broke it off at the base. He cleaned off all the shoots and branches except for one near the base which he broke leaving about four inches attached. He held it up. It looked like a miniature stilt, but I knew Father would not have created anything for a frivolous purpose.

"This is how you use it," he said, going back to the ridge he had just fashioned out of the scrawny earth. Putting his foot on the short butt of the horizontal branch, he drove the stick down into the ground, joggled it around, and pulled it up again. "There you are," said he, "the perfect size for a seed potato." And he dropped down a half potato by way of demonstration. "Not too difficult, is it?"

I took to the stick, and tackled the ridge with gusto, puncturing it with gaping holes, three across, as Father had directed. When I fed each open mouth with a seed, a sliver of a potato with an eye sprouting the merest suggestion of a bud, Father came along behind scooping more earth out of the furrow to cover the holes.

So this was how they cultivated the sides of the mountains back home. Straightening my back I gave an involuntary glance towards the northwest where the last light of the day was concentrated behind Sliabh Bawn. No more than a hill, it was called the 'white mountain' as if it were permanently covered with snow, like Mount Everest. Still it was always the point on the horizon that drew my gaze, and that last glow of twilight behind it fascinated me, seeming to settle on a distant Tireragh until the darkness finally snuffed it out.

"A bit of manure on top here will have these lads jumping out of the ground," said Father bringing down the flat back of the shovel on the ridge as if he were trying to squash any urge to grow the poor potatoes might have had.

"Where will we get manure? We can't go to the sea for wrack here."

"No, we won't be wading up to our oxters in the sea salvaging wrack. That's what I saved you from, young fellow. That's what we're running a hundred miles from. Don't forget it."

"Was it worse than what the men were doing down around the bagger."

"They're paid for working on the bog. They're guaranteed their cheques every Thursday. That's better than humping wrack, or humping slatamaras out of the tide, hoping you will get them dry, hoping that the man will give you a few bob for them."

"Still."

"Still nothing. Here there will be schools and jobs. If you work hard at school there will be no need for you to go humping slatamaras, or following the bagger for that matter. You can be swanking around in a collar and tie, in a Sunday suit, like the best of them."

"But do you not miss it?"

"Miss what? Sligo?" He stood up and like me glanced at the bright clouds over Sliabh Bawn, silent for a moment. "I'll tell you what. The footing will be coming up in the summer. There's good money to be made at the footing, and anyone can do a bit. So if we have a go, and earn some money, we'll hire a lorry and go back for a bit of a holiday before the end of the summer. How would you like that?"

I was breathless. Until that moment I had existed between the hope that we would one day gather our belongings and return to Sligo, and the despair that we would never again lay eyes on that promised land. Here was a middle way, a different possibility.

"That would be great," I managed to gasp.

"Yeah, I thought you might like that. Now, why don't you ramble up to Jim and ask him if he would have a load or two of dung he would sell us."

Normally my bashfulness would have made such a chore excruciating, but this time I skipped up with the confidence of one who has been handed the key to the Garden of Eden.

Jim lived in a small cottage with a galvanised iron roof. Around the cottage was an intimate little farmyard with a few sheds for the animals and poultry. The door was open and the interior dimly lit. Jim was sitting beside the fire engaged in the task of lighting his pipe. When he had it lit he placed a round steel perforated cap on the top of it, and sat back, clearly enjoying the satisfaction of the smoke and the prospect of conversation.

"Tell me now, how is the tillage going?" he asked.

"Not bad. It was hard to plough, so we couldn't get drills in it. But we're laying it out in ridges."

"There's nothing wrong with ridges." Jim gathered his shoulders a little, as if criticism had been implied. "Weren't we making ridges long before the ploughs came along?"

"Yes, but it means we'll have to dig them by hand too." I urged my point, as I had heard Father clarify the consequences. "We won't be able to get in a digger."

"You're as well off, son. Those machines destroy the spuds. They cut lumps out of every second one. I wouldn't let them near a field myself. If you dig them by hand you'll get every last spud out of the ground."

"Yeah," I said only too aware of how much extra work it would involve for Father, and no doubt for me.

"By the way, don't tell herself about our deal on the conacre. I like to keep my business to myself, if you know what I mean."

"Herself?"

"The missus. She's not here this evening, but when she bumps into you around the place, she'll be quizzing you up and down. But say nothing, do you hear?"

"Alright."

Jim sat back in silence, whatever anxiety he might have had now allayed, puffing away at his steel-capped pipe.

"Is it true that you make up poems and recitations, Jim?"

"It is."

"Can I see one? Have you any written out?"

"I don't write them out. I make them up in my head and then I say them."

Father had brought back a story about the Shan, that a publican had once challenged him on his ability to compose his own recitations, claiming he was merely repeating ones he had picked up elsewhere. Jim took up the challenge and invited the publican to pledge a pint of stout for everyone in the bar on the outcome. The pints were pledged and an excited audience gathered around. The publican demanded that he compose a poem or recitation which would be clearly original. Jim assured him that he would have no difficulty recognising the originality of his effort. He then went to the toilet. When he returned he delivered a recitation about an incident in which the publican himself was unflatteringly involved. After that no one challenged Jim on the authenticity of his composition.

"Would you like to hear one?" he asked.

"Yeah, I would."

He took the pipe from his mouth, cleared his throat and spat into the fire, then recited a scathing satire on a family whose members were constantly borrowing, but never repaying. I began to shift uneasily on my chair. Clearly the Shan was not one to be antagonised.

"My father was wondering if you would have a load of dung for sale." I thought it wise to complete my business and make good my escape lest I become the subject of one of his poems and be the laughing stock of the parish.

"No, I haven't," replied Jim. "But I'll tell you who has. Charlie Rhatigan. He's the next house up on the other side of the road."

When I told Father of Jim's anxiety to keep his transactions secret from his wife, he guffawed. "He's a holy terror. You'll find he's up to something. He'll probably sell the spuds and vegetables to her at an exorbitant price. She's the one who does the bit of farming and holds the purse. One time she had reared a nice heifer, and asked Jim to take it to the fair and sell it for her. Jim did that and got a very good price, forty pounds. When he arrived home the wife asked him how much did he get? 'Guess,' said he. 'You should have got thirty five pounds anyway,' she said. 'Ah, someone told you. You must have been talking to someone,' said Jim reaching into his pocket and counting out thirty five pounds."

"He hasn't any dung to sell, but he said we might get some in the next house up, from a man called Charlie

Rhatigan."

"Right. We'll head up there now as soon as I have this ridge finished."

Charlie Rhatigan's house was a thatched cottage at right angles to the road. It appeared very long because there were two stables in the same row as the house. We walked up the yard to his front door, which was open. The kitchen was dark, lit by a single electric bulb suspended from a rafter in the centre of the roof.

Charlie was there, sitting down to his supper. He grunted a polite greeting, but didn't get up to fuss as most people would have done. He waved his hand to where there were empty chairs beside the fire. We sat down, stretching our shins towards the blazing sods of turf and absorbed the heat as if we had come just for this, while Charlie finished off eating his meal. We waited in silence until he pulled over his chair.

"You've started working down in the Shan's field, I see." His farm was on a height so he probably had vantage over the neighbouring farms.

"We have," said Father, sounding as relieved as I felt, that the uncomfortable silence was over.

"You're starting early, but you're well advised. You'll be hard pressed to get a crop out of that field."

My heart sank every time I heard this judgement, as if we had been taken-in by the guile of the Shan.

"Why is it so contrary?" asked Father.

Charlie paused for a moment, contemplating the fire. "It's all reclaimed land down there. About forty years ago they cleared the scrub and drained it. But the roots take a long time to decompose in the boggy soil."

"I've worked hungrier soil back home," said Father.

"I hope he's not charging you much for it."

"No, he's decent enough on that score. All he wants is a few bags of spuds."

"Just as well. You're doing him a favour digging it up and turning it over. It'll be good land in about another generation." Charlie allowed himself the faintest hint of a smile.

46

"We're looking for a couple of loads of dung."

"A couple of cart-loads?"

"That should be adequate."

"I have a couple of cart-loads to spare. Do you have a cart?"

"No."

"When do you want it?"

"Whenever. Maybe Saturday."

"Alright if you come up on Saturday after the dinner, I'll tackle the horse and you can take two loads from the pit at the top of the yard."

Silence set in now that the business was done, the three of us gazing at the dancing flames of the fire over our outstretched legs.

"I notice you have a lot of hens around the place." Father eventually broke the silence. "Do you have eggs for sale?"

"I do," said Charlie. "How many do you want?"

"Would you have ten shillings worth?"

"I might have."

"Every week?"

"That's an awful lot of eggs."

"We have an awful lot of mouths to feed."

"Alright, I'll keep ten shillings worth for you every week, and I'll give them to you at the wholesale price. They're still a bit scarce and a bit dear, but they'll be getting plentiful coming towards the summer."

"That's fine. I'll send Robbie here to collect them every Sunday after Mass."

There was a weight in the pit of my stomach as we got up to leave. The prospect of dealing with Charlie on my own was not attractive. He had hardly acknowledged my presence all the while we were in his kitchen, and his brooding reticence filled me with unease. Still, cheap eggs were cheap eggs, and I was keen to assist in any economy measure, now that Father had unveiled the unspeakable vision of going back to Sligo for a holiday.

47

9

I was reminded today how much you missed the sea. You missed other things too of course, the people above all, the chapel bell from the village of Easkey echoing over the fields on a Sunday morning, the sally shoots waving across Maloneys' wall. But when you lay sleepless in your single bed in the front room in Ballyclare, it was for the sound of the sea you were straining your ears.

I hear it now. It is a constant low murmur, too delicate, too natural to impinge on the silence. It was in your ears from the day you were born till the day you left. The silence of the Midlands was an empty silence by comparison.

Yes, today I recalled your ache and your straining. I jokingly asked the builder if they still drew sand from the bunkers on the Cimin. He replied that that facility had been barred long ago. He added that builders had always been reluctant to use sand drawn from the shore anyway, that it was inclined to moisten and weep at full tide.

He was serious. And I recalled the ache of your separation in the weeping sand.

10

The cross was a natural meeting point and loitering area for the children of The Park, and there were children in almost every one of the sixty-four houses. There were many boys of my age and we congregated around the cross in the evenings after the chores were complete or on Sundays after the mid-day dinner.

On such a Sunday afternoon, sitting on the concrete plinth of the cross, we were debating how we would spend the luxurious hours of freedom that stretched before us. Would it be a game of football on the playing field, or Cowboys and Indians across the wire fence in Gillen's field?

"Why don't we go and explore the wood?" suggested Val Brennan.

"The little one, or the big one?" asked Paddy O'Donnell.

"The big one, of course. What's there to explore in the little one?"

"It would take ages," said Paddy. "We'd probably be late home for the tea, and they'd be sending the Guards out to look for us."

The four of us turned to look down over the Shannon and out to Lough Ree. The cross was well placed for the country to see, and so the whole country was there to be viewed from the base of the cross. The big wood swept down towards the shore of the river. It was tempting. We paused to think.

Val was the most recent arrival in The Park and, having come from Dublin, displayed the ease and confidence one would expect only of a local. No one could understand why a family would leave Dublin for a place like Ballyclare, why a man with the choice of all the attractive jobs in the city would choose to work for the Turf Company. When the question was put to Val's father, he said it was the fresh air and the fishing. None of us believed that, since fresh air did not rate on anybody else's list of desirables, and the man stood alone when he cast out from under the bridge for the fresh-water fish no one would eat.

"Alright then, why don't we all go home, say we're going down to the big wood to collect sticks for the fire and that we might be late getting back." His Dublin accent added a touch of authority to his words and we agreed. The fact that Val's father was a turner and operated some mysterious machine called a lathe seemed also to add to Val's superior knowledge of the world.

Paddy O'Donnell came from Donegal and Art McHugh from Erris in Co. Mayo. Their fathers were labourers on the bog. They both had red hair and freckles, and were often taken for brothers. But the resemblance was all on the surface: Paddy was lively, talkative, sociable, whereas Art was extremely quiet.

When we re-grouped on the play-green we set off across Gillen's field. This huge wild stretch of land ran from the wired boundary of The Park down to the High Road. Bushes grew at random throughout the field. Everywhere the surface was punctured by outcrops of grey rock that had a skin rashed and scabbed and pock-marked from age and weather and the growth of lichens. We loved that field. There were evenings when all the children of The Park invaded it like a tribe of Indians intent on reclaiming it from the White Man. With so many bunkers and boulders it was ideal for the long gun-battles that raged to and fro until the White Man in the person of the irate farmer, John Gillen, appeared and routed the Indians who beat a hasty retreat back to the wired confines of the reservation.

We didn't pause now to play Cowboys and Indians. We were off to explore a new frontier, with our bits of rope wound importantly over one shoulder and under the oxter of the other.

Once we crossed the High Road we were into the big wood. It was an absolute thicket of small trees and bushes, ash, birch, and hazel being most prolific. But we found paths through the thicket even though we still had to

50

squeeze our way along. Deep in the wood we came across the incongruous mass of a Scots pine towering above us.

"If we get lost we can climb that tree and see our way out," said Val.

"We can't get lost. The slope is all downhill to the river, all uphill to the road," replied Paddy.

Val was disappointed. He had clearly been anticipating the excitement of getting lost and resorting to heroics to extricate ourselves from the grasp of the forest.

And so we pushed on downhill until suddenly the wood drew back, light flowed around us, and we were standing on the shore of the river. Indeed the river at this place was more of a lake where it swelled out before running through a narrow gut into Lough Ree. But facing us was not an expanse of water but banks of reeds.

"Down here somewhere must be where the sand-beds are," said Paddy.

We had heard the local boys talking of the sand-beds where they went bathing and picnicking in the summer. We moved along the reedy shore of the river and sure enough the wood peeled back a little to leave a grassy bank. Then we stumbled on what had to be the sand-beds, nothing like the Atlantic beaches but nevertheless little pockets of sand on the shore and under the water where the banks of reeds rolled back to leave a natural bathing pool.

"This will be a great place to come in the summer," said Val. "We can bring picnics and go bathing in the river."

"We can swim," interjected Art excitedly. It was so seldom he spoke that we instinctively paused to listen when he did. However, when attention was focussed on him he got self-conscious and embarrassed and usually clammed up again. Not this time - his excitement lifted over his inhibition.

"I don't know how to swim," said Val.

"Me neither," added Paddy. "What about you Robbie?"

"No."

"I do. I can teach you," said Art. We had never seen such enthusiasm in him before.

"Where did you learn?" asked Val.

"Back home in Erris. We had a teacher who made us all go down to this little pool by the sea called Poll Gorm. It was a stranded pool when the tide was out, so it was dead safe. He always said he would teach every child in Erris to swim if it was the last thing he did, on account of so many being drowned off the boats. Master Lavelle was his name."

"But if people were out in boats all the time, were they not able to swim?" asked Val.

"No. That was the point. Until Master Lavelle came along, no one knew how to swim. They thought it was better not to be able to swim. That way, if the boat capsized, the end came quicker."

"Jeeze," said Val. "You mean they deliberately didn't learn to swim so they would drown quicker if they fell out of the boat?"

"That's right," said Art, now hanging his head a little, and blushing, clearly embarrassed that he was portraying his own people in an unfavourable light.

Paddy recognised his plight and joined in. "How did he teach you to swim?"

Art brightened again. "We had all these tubes, old car tubes, bicycle tubes, all blown up. He would start us off with big car tubes under us, teaching us the strokes. After we had learned the strokes and got used to the water, we had to let some of the air out of the tube. We changed to bicycle tubes when we got fairly good, and in the end we could swim without any tube at all."

"And he brought you down during school time?" asked Paddy, his eyes wide with disbelief.

"Sometimes, on a good day, coming up to the summer holidays, but it was mostly after school. Still he made sure we all came down. If someone tried to get out of it, he would go to his parents and read them out of it. They were all afraid of Master Lavelle, so they didn't cross him. My old fellow was always giving out, that it was all codology, that we would be better occupied helping with the farm work at that time of the year. But still he let me go. It was great."

"Fair dues to Master Lavelle," said Val. "Come the summer we'll get some tubes and come down here. You can teach us to swim."

"Yeah, okay," nodded Art, clearly pleased in his quiet way.

"We'd better start gathering our sticks, or we'll be right late getting back," advised Paddy.

We made our way back along the shore and when we saw the towering pine tree we made our way towards it, then up the slope until we were close to the road. There we found a little clearing and laid out our ropes on the ground. Quickly we gathered up some of the dead branches that were strewn everywhere and laid them on the ropes. When we had as much as we could carry we tied up the bundles, threw them on our shoulders and headed back towards The Park across Gillen's field.

11

The 'why' continued to trouble you, didn't it? You listened to Father's justifications. There was logic there, right enough. Too much logic, perhaps. Was he trying to give a reasonable appearance to that which was driven by emotion or mood? I'm not sure either, even now.

His arguments about schools and jobs were foreseeing enough. The schools were more convenient in Ballyclare, but they weren't that remote in Tireragh. The development of the bogs certainly brought more jobs and the enterprise culture to the Midlands. But the pale of success still circled Dublin. So why?

Was it the overwhelming burden of the deaths of his brothers and sisters in rapid succession from TB? Was he afraid the consumption would extend to you, and Eileen and Mikey and the others? Was he running from the stigma of the consumptive family?

He was worshipped in Tireragh for his prowess on the football field. He brought glory to his parish and served his county well. So why? Was it that matter of honour? From the time I heard of it I assumed it explained everything. But once, when we were enjoying a drink together, I sprang it on him. He reacted sharply. He said it wasn't the matter of honour or dishonour that affected him most. His path had crossed the perpetrator's on Easkey Bridge. Words led to punches, and he would have chucked the man over the parapet had he not managed to wriggle out of his jacket. He ran for his life, and Father was left standing on the bridge, in his hands the empty jacket, which he dispatched unceremoniously into the river. One slither of a snake was all that had stood between him and murder.

12

"We might find the bones of an old Dane down here," Father joked. He was tossing the sods of wet peat up to me from the bottom spit of the turf bank. This bottom layer must have been about twelve foot down from the surface and he was touching the gravel underneath, but the peat there was compressed and black and would provide the best fuel so he was anxious to dig it all out.

It was getting dark and shadow was thickening in the bog-hole. Father's clothes and face were black from his day's work in the forge, so that when he swung upwards with the slane to toss the sod into my hands, all I saw clearly was the white of his eyes.

"It's a lot deeper than the bogs at home," I ventured, hoping for a pause in the relentless flow of sods. My job was not particularly heavy. I dropped the sods on top of the flat turf-barrow and when it was full I wheeled it away and tipped the sods out on the bank where they would be left to dry.

"Ay," was all he said.

It was not easy to divert Father into conversation, and it was not easy to get him reminiscing. There was a block, a stone wall much of the time between him and the past. He seemed to dream only of the future, in the way that my magnetic needle always rotated towards the past, towards the north-west. Every time I tipped a load, I paused to gaze at the last of the light fading over Sliabh Bawn.

Father and the village of Ballyclare were well matched, both careering towards the future as if there had been no yesterday. There were new shops opening, people setting up in their own homes services such as hairdressing, sewing, and the like. Someone had converted an old shed on the main street into a cinema and was showing cowboy films, like 'Shane' and sword-fighting films, like 'The Three Musketeers.' Now, a completely new cinema was being built just off the main street, and the owner, Johnny Kenny, had offered Paddy and Val jobs at half-a-crown a night. Not bad when the rest of us would have to pay sixpence to see the film. They would be showing people to their seats, and sweeping out the hall afterwards. But Johnny had promised to train them on the projectors and that was the most exciting aspect of it.

I would have enjoyed that job, so much better than weeding potatoes, or thinning carrots, or setting cabbage plants. And three half crowns a week would help to buy things. It was always the hardest time of the year, coming into the summer. And now, because our stocks had run out, we had to buy potatoes and vegetables in the shop. Meat we could afford only every second day; every other day it was 'bruitin', mashed potatoes with chopped onions through it, mixed with milk and butter. Occasionally Mother would surprise us with a tin of baked beans.

Yes, it was a lean time, and a few extra half-crowns would make a difference. Mother never failed to hand out sixpence each to Eileen, Mikey, and myself to go to the pictures on a Sunday night, so I would be saving her money there too if I could see the film for free.

I had been pondering how to draw down the subject with Father. Now when he was hidden from me like the priest in a confessional box, I grasped the opportunity.

"Paddy and Val are going to work in the new cinema." I tried to sound nonchalant as I caught another sod and tossed it on to the barrow.

"Are they? And what will they be doing?"

"Just helping around the place at first, taking up the tickets, sweeping out the hall, that sort of thing."

"Well that shouldn't be beyond them."

"After a while they will be trained to work the projectors, and they will take turns showing the films."

"They'll enjoy that."

"They will. He might be taking on someone else as well. I

wouldn't mind a job like that."

"You have enough to do. There's plenty of work on the crops, and by the time we have these turf saved you'll have had your fill of work."

"But I could manage alright. The pictures don't start until eight o'clock, and it's only three nights a week."

"Only three nights a week! And what about your homework? Would you go neglecting that?"

"I could manage, honestly. It would be no bother."

"Look, young fellow, forget about the pictures. The only thing I want you to concentrate on is your schoolwork. You're able to learn, and if you do well at school, you'll go places, believe me."

"I know that and I like schoolwork. I wouldn't neglect it."

A note of desperation and pleading had entered my voice, betraying how intensely I wanted to join my friends swaggering about the cinema. It was that which drew the anger from Father.

"For frig's sake, will you lay off. I won't have any son of mine working for another man. You don't know how lucky you are. You don't realise what a chance you're getting. My father took me out of school when I was your age, or younger. He took me out of school to put me working for this buck of a farmer down the road. I worked like a slave, and at the end of the year this farmer singled out a young bullock from the field, and my father came to drive him home. That was the pay-off he got for my year's hard labour. I swore then I would get on. But, by God, I had to do it the hard way. I had to work five years for nothing in order to serve my time as a blacksmith. And I mean nothing, not as much as a red penny did I get. You have a chance of doing better and doing it easier, so concentrate on your school lessons and forget about the pictures."

I knew there was no point in further argument. I could do my school lessons blindfolded, and enjoyed doing them, so I could not understand why he got so worked up.

The sods were coming at twice the pace now, and I had ferried out several barrowfuls before he paused again.

"There will be plenty of opportunity to earn money when the summer comes. Do you see all the turf the Company has cut? That has to be footed as soon as it's dry. There will be plenty of work there for everyone. And you'll be employed by the Company."

I looked out over the expanse of cut turf left behind by the bagger in neat rows, in geometric lines, stretching to the horizon miles away. By comparison our hand-cut turf spread in random disarray looked crude and insignificant. The bank we were cutting in the age-old style was on the margin of the bog. When the Company took over this vast tract they had to leave an apron all around the edge in the possession of the local farmers so that they could continue to harvest their own fuel in the traditional way. It was from one of these farmers that we had rented the turf-bank.

When Father had tossed up the last sod from the bottom spit, he quickly began to clamber out of the bog-hole. I could hear his wellingtons squelching in the water which was rapidly moving in to claim the space.

On top of the bank he stood beside me looking at the sods I had scattered with the turf-barrow, then at the expanse of the Company's turf.

"There will be plenty of work there for the summer, and plenty of money to be made. And when the summer is over, before you all go back to school, we will take off for Sligo."

13

Wheels come full circle, they say. And the cliché brings me out to the garden in search of the granite base where Father used to shoe the timber cartwheels. Do you remember the glowing round band of iron he took from the fire with the long-handled tongs? How he eased it over the rim of the naked wheel and sledge-hammered it into place?

There is no sign of the base. The earth has eased itself over it. It lies beneath somewhere, like so much more, like Father, like the men who stood around, admiring the craftsman and his craft, now awaiting the resurrection or the archaeologist's trowel. Even the forge is no more.

But the house still stands, and I have redeemed it, finally. I kept your promise. I kept my promise to Anthony as well, and hoped it would compel him from his sick bed to complete the dream. How many times in smoky bars in faraway cities did we meet and dream of being back in Killeenduff, side-by-side again? Anthony, who had the gift of turning blocks of stone into objects of unspeakable beauty. You expected success of Anthony. He was like that from the beginning, always committed utterly, not to some notion of a career but to whatever project was in front of him. Even as he lay in his sick bed he was obsessed with a work which would manifest his predicament in image and symbol. He was not one to lie down, even in his sick bed.

I didn't realise his magical powers were forsaking him when he told me of his difficulties in carving the Blacksmith. His last carved sculpture was of Father in his blacksmith's apron, his powerful arms plunging the tongs and seething metal into the cooling trough. It now adorns a park in a town Father never even visited.

I have been browsing over the deeds. It is curious to see

how our two fathers built the houses on the one plot, a strip of woodland left behind when the farmland was all annexed from the old landlord and distributed among the local farmers. Born within a year of one another, you knew Anthony from the time you could walk, and you grew into boyhood together, cousins, playmates, next-door neighbours. Anthony and I also grew into manhood together, into age, like twin brothers, soul-mates. How often in those smoky bars, after we had talked through our abiding interests, art and writing, would we turn to the subject that set us both aglow, Killeenduff, Tireragh. After perhaps marvelling at Le Corbusier's use of the Golden Section, we would proceed to debate the places we used to find the sweetest vetches growing, and recall how once, when we were herding geese on the Wrack Road, we discovered a rich crop tucked under a clump of briars, how we relished the miniscule peas when we popped the ripe pods.

Anthony would always admonish me to retrieve the old house. And then we would sit back in silence, dreaming.

Yes, I have now retrieved the house. Retrieving the past is a different matter.

14

There was a clump of ferns on the edge of the Company's service yard, screening the bank where our hand-cut turf lay scattered higgledy-piggledy. I was lurking in these high ferns waiting in expectation for Father. Today was the day. This was the big event. The Company had declared that their turf was ready for footing.

For weeks little else had been talked about. The men who had been around in previous years were explaining how the plots were taken, and secured. Their descriptions gave me an impression of a great race similar to the ones in the cowboy films where a new state was being opened up, and the settlers lined up by the thousand on the frontier. On the discharge of a single shot, they were off, hell-for-leather, to claim and secure the best tract of land they could find.

There was speculation as to how much money a single man could earn, and how much he could earn if he had children to help him. The accepted opinion was that a child, being closer to the ground and not having to bend his back, could do almost as much as a man.

I was to meet Father at this spot as soon as he finished work. Hiding in the ferns, I gave occasional glances at the dark entrance to the forge, watching the wagons on the tip-head being heeled over, one after another, into the expectant lorries underneath. Every time a load fell there was a thunderous rattle and a cloud of turf mould puffed up out of the lorry. Most of the lorries had 'McHenry' written on them and I knew their cargo was destined for the Dublin market.

Eventually the hooter sounded and I saw Father emerge from the mouth of the forge as if he had been waiting for the starting pistol. He had his lunch-bag slung over his shoulder and his coat under one arm. In the other hand he held a billy-can down by his side. As always his face was black from the coal-dust of the forge, and that accentuated his eyes where all the expression was concentrated.

I waved at him and he came straight towards me across the yard.

"First things first," he said, and sat down in the clump of ferns beside me. He placed the billy-can carefully on the ground. It was filled to the brim with steaming tea, drawn to a dark brown heavy consistency, as Father liked it. I opened the bag I had brought and took out the clean mugs and the sandwiches that Mother had packed. We sat back and feasted like lords as if we had met for this sole purpose. And, although I had to suck the tea through my teeth to strain off the abundance of tea leaves, it had that wonderful flavour of the outdoors that transformed even the most ordinary of food.

"I think we're right now," said Father as soon as we had finished eating. "They say an empty bag won't stand up, but we don't want to be too full for the job we're going to, or we won't be able to bend." And he laughed at his little joke. He was clearly in good form.

We made our way the short distance to the bottom of Trench Three where the footing had begun that morning. Already the even geometry of the spread turf was utterly disrupted. Everywhere there were patches of dark brown footings rising out of the light brown plane.

And there were people, hundreds of them strung out down along the bank as far the eye could see, men, women, children. The bright colours of their clothes stood out in lively contrast to the dark bog, and suggested gaiety. To my admiring gaze it had almost the appearance of a carnival.

But their backs were bent and they didn't raise their heads to greet us as we walked along the top of the bank. Father pointed out to me how the rows of turf had been divided into plots, a timber lath with a number on it marking the beginning of each new plot. Each person secured a plot by putting up a few footings on the top row. Some must have started early that morning because they had already substantial parts of the early plots footed.

After walking about a quarter of a mile past this motley work force we came to the place where only a row or two had been footed, suggesting the plots had been newly taken. Then we arrived where only the spread turf stretched ahead of us. Father laid his coat and bag on the dry turf clamp and surveyed the first vacant plot. I did likewise.

He pointed out the lath which marked the first row of the plot. There were strange markings on the turf where the lath was planted. He laughed when I asked him what they were.

"We call that the 'crow's foot'. The gangers put that mark down where they place the lath so that it can't be moved. Before this a sly boy would shift the lath to add an extra couple of rows of turf to his neighbour's plot and save himself the bother of footing them."

"But that's cheating. Why would he do that?"

"You'll find, when it comes down to money, that people are capable of doing anything. So keep your eyes open, and let no one pull a fast one on you."

I looked down the bog at the array of stooped backs. In some plots there were men working alone, but in others whole families were at work, a man and a woman with three or four children. Nothing could look more innocent. Father was already erecting the proprietary footings.

"How much will we get for doing this plot?" I asked him.

"Good money. If we do two of these plots we'll earn as much as I get working in the forge for a week."

He opened up another row for me, demonstrating how to do the footings in the way required by the Company. These footings differed from the style used with hand-cut turf. The traditional method was to prop two sods upright supporting one another then to add another five or six all upright all leaning against one another for support but with enough space between them to allow air to circulate. On top of this little clump two or three more sods would be placed lengthways, totally clear of the ground. However, the Company's sods were longer and thinner and harder than the hand-cut ones. And the new style of footing was simpler. You put two sods on the ground well apart, then two more crossways on top of them, two more crossways again until it was six to eight layers high. With the wide gaps between the sods and the hollow centre there was plenty of ventilation through the footing.

"You have to keep the footings in a straight line so that people can walk through them." Father said, going back to his own row and allowing me to continue with the second row he had opened.

"High windows," he said.

"What?"

"High windows – that's what they call this type of footing."

"Is that a nick-name, or is that what the Company calls it?"

"I don't know. They just call them high windows."

It was easy to see why, with the gaps that you could look through into the centre of the footing. Father was popping them up at a great rate and moving ahead of me down through the spread of turf from top to bottom, taking three rows of the double sods in front of him and leaving a single neat row of footings behind him. I tried to emulate him, but I found it slow and tedious, two sods across two sods across two sods. By the time I had raised about ten footings, I realised that there was a frightful lot of turf in a row, not to mind the nineteen rows of footings that would make up the plot.

"How do you find it?" asked Father straightening up.

"It's slow."

"Well, take it easy. Don't go killing yourself. Let your back get used to the bending and in no time you will be well able for it."

I looked at the few footings I had put up in the row behind me. It was pitiful, and yet he was telling me to take it easy. Down along the bank there was nothing but bent backs showing; even the women and children were sticking to their task, and I marvelled, considering that some of them must have been working from morning.

64

I stayed watching to see how long they continued without straightening up for a rest. I was amazed. There was no easing off for any of them.

"How can they keep going without taking a rest?" I asked Father as he approached me again, coming back on his second row.

He stood up and looked at the motley ranks working furiously. "They're probably thinking of the money they will get when they finish the plot. That's a good anaesthetic." He laughed and resumed footing. "Or it might be that their backs are so sore when they straighten up, they find it easier to stay bent."

I had reached the half-way stage in my row, or thereabouts, and felt some sense of achievement. I took a stroll down across the spread turf to the bottom, counting the sods that I had yet to foot, then went back and counted the ones I had done to verify that I had actually reached the half-way mark.

When Father saw me walking around he lifted his head. "There's a couple of sandwiches left in the bag, and a drop of milk. Do you want to bring them down and we'll finish them off?"

I was delighted to. And we stretched ourselves out on the crisp dry backs of the spread turf, munching the crushed sandwiches, passing the milk bottle between us. The food tasted exotic, like a feast prepared for a king. Yes, food always tasted better in the open air, but when eating was an alternative to work, the taste was more exquisite still.

"We'll do a bit every evening like this, and a bit on Saturday. There's no use in killing ourselves. When you get the summer holidays, yourself and maybe even Eileen and Mikey can come out every day. I'll keep coming out in the evenings after work. We'll get a few plots done, and collect our few bob."

"How will they pay us?"

"When the plot is finished the ganger will make a note in his book. They will put the money through into my cheque, so I should have it about a fortnight later."

"Who's the ganger?"

"I don't know who's on this trench, but we'll know soon enough. You'll see him prancing up and down, trying to look important. But keep on the right side of him, whoever he is. Those gobshites can make life very difficult for you if they take a turn against you."

"I'll watch out for them."

"And agree with them, whatever they say. They don't like to be contradicted or taken on. Even if they're cribbing about something, nod your head. They want people to acknowledge how important they are, how much they've come on in the world. You know the way. And if they think they have impressed you, they'll probably pass no more heed of what you're doing."

"I know. Everybody talks about Long Paddy McEvoy. He used to cycle out to work with the rest of the men, and back in the evening as well. But after he was made a ganger, he took to leaving earlier and cycling out by himself. Silly eejit."

"He might be a silly eegit," said Father, laughing, "but to you he's not Long Paddy, he's Mr. McEvoy. Now do you think you'd be able to finish that row tonight. The minute you have it done, we'll pack up and leave."

"Okay." And I got up with a spring.

15

Do you remember the crowd that gathered the day you left? Men, women, children. The children, mostly cousins, first second third, looked on silently, a portion of their playmates being erased at the one stroke. The women, helping Mother with the last of the packing, carried boxes of utensils, folded blankets, bundles of clothes, out to the back of the lorry.

You helped to put them aboard. Then someone handed you the shoe box with the football medals, all clinking inside, and you didn't know where to place it. How could you lob such a tabernacle on to the back of the lorry? You lifted the battered lid and ran your finger through the shining silver disks, touched the gold at the heart of the most substantial ones, Sligo Champions, Connaught League Champions. Some were duplicated, and belonged to your dead uncles. Missing was the All-Ireland medal your uncle had won. That was lost, like so much more, in the aftermath of his death.

You were roused out of your reverie by a shout from Father. He, Josie Connor, and Red Lavelle were about to heave the anvil up on to the back of the lorry. There were tears rolling down Red's face. Josie Connor was silent and serious, he who was never without a smile on his face or a joke on the tip of his tongue, he who had brought you on the bar of his bike to see Duffys' Circus on the Fairgreen in Dromore West. You could watch no longer.

On the pretext of taking the box of medals to a safer place, you abandoned your post and took refuge in the cab. You sat there, not daring to look at the pain in people's faces, the men, the women, even the silent children. You stared up the road you must go, past the Split Rock, over Kilcullen's hill.

Then the door of the cab swung open. Anthony clambered up beside you. What did he say? What did you say? I can't recall. But you sat there together, staring up the road until all was loaded behind.

And the ghosts of all those people are around me now, sitting on the low wall outside, neighbours Bridgie and Katie Maloney, Mike and Charlie. They lived out their time quietly around this corner, their lives as natural as those of the sycamore trees. Why did they grieve that day? Was it for us or for themselves? Is there something within us permanently setting us at odds with the easy blossoming of the fuchsia?

And what should I be doing now? Retrieving the past? Re-creating it? Giving voice to those silent ghosts? Can I make a single daisy grow again, or a single blackbird warble a reprise?

16

My Sunday afternoon trips out to Charlie Rhatigan's to collect the weekly supply of eggs had started as a chore but soon became a treat. After Mass I grabbed a shopping bag, mounted the bike, and pedalled out the couple of miles to his house.

His dour manner never changed, his gruff greeting, his awkward silence while I wrapped the eggs in the torn-up pages of the Farmers' Journal. In spite of all that I had a sense of a great warmth underneath, a sense that there was real worth hidden behind his austere faÇade.

Once, when I approached his open front door, I was taken aback by the sound of laughter. At first I thought he had company. I listened. There was no conversation, just the sound of the radio, which was blaring a familiar comedy programme. Then came another gust of laughter. I realised it was Charlie, laughing at every contrived joke, laughing with total merry abandonment. I was reluctant to intrude, but I could hardly turn away; neither could I remain like a perplexed rabbit and risk being caught eavesdropping. So I made some noise with my feet and approached the door slowly. Of course he clammed the moment I entered and assumed his cloak of reserve.

Whether I betrayed in my manner that I had glimpsed him in an unfamiliar light, or whether his habitual humour had been disoriented by the comedy programme, or whether he was unnerved by the way I was glancing into his eyes to find the lightness he tried so hard to conceal, I do not know. But he surprised me again by going down to the room and coming back with a book, the biggest book I had ever seen. He held it with both hands and placed it on the table in front of me. There was a heavy brown leather cover on it with gold lettering so faded I could not decipher the title.

Charlie opened the book. From inside the cover he took a tattered yellow press cutting and placed it in front of me.

"Do you recognise that house?" he asked, pointing to the image of a thatched cottage at the head of the newspaper article.

I looked carefully. It was just another thatched cottage to me. I saw no distinctive features. I read the caption, hoping for a clue. 'The house where Fr. Joseph Mullooly was born.' Mullooly was a local name, but still I could not identify the house.

"What will you be when you grow up?" Charlie enquired.

"I don't know."

"Well, rule out being a detective anyway."

"Why."

"Because you're sitting in that house right now."

"Really?"

"Yes, really."

I glanced down through the newspaper article. It was a biographical piece on a Father Mullooly who had pioneered archaeology in Rome. He had been the prior of a church called St. Clement's and had a feeling that it was built on top of an old Basilica built by St. Clement himself in the early years of the Church in Rome. So he started excavating. Not only did he find St. Clement's Basilica, but he found the ruins of an old Roman temple beneath that again. It was such an astonishing discovery that all the monarchs of Europe came visiting to see it and admire it.

I was impressed. I had never encountered fame before, not the kind of fame that is documented in newspapers. I studied the picture of the house again. Gradually I began to recognise some distinguishing features even though it was clear that the photograph had been taken a long time previously.

I opened the book and turned to the title page. It was written by the same Reverend Joseph Mullooly and it was an account of his archaeological project.

"Can I borrow it?"

"That book hasn't left this house since it arrived nearly a

hundred years ago."

"But I'd like to read it."

"Then you'll have to read it here."

I turned to the first page and started to read, but every second word I couldn't understand.

"The words are very hard. Have you read it?"

"I'm not a scholar. But I think you have the makings of one."

"Why do you say that?"

Charlie looked at me and I detected a suppressed smile on his face. "For one thing, you wear glasses."

"But that's because I'm short-sighted."

"Aren't you that way from reading books?"

"Only school books. And the comics my friend gets from America. Have you any more books?"

"Only that one. What would I be doing with books?"

"You've kept this one for a hundred years."

"That's different. He was my great grand uncle, and he was born in this house. I was born here too, and I inherited the house, the farm, and the book. When my mother was dying, she put more store on passing the book on to me than the house and farm. I'm sure she never read it. Neither did I. But still it's as if without it the sun wouldn't rise or the grass grow or the hens lay their eggs. That's the way it's been with us."

"Like the O'Donnells."

"Which O'Donnells would they be?"

"The O'Donnells in Donegal, you know, the famous O'Donnells."

"Oh, those O'Donnells."

"They had St.Colmcille's book, the oldest book in Ireland, and every time they went into battle they brought the book with them. They believed that while they had the book they could never be defeated."

"I know how they felt. Who told you that story?"

"It's not a story, it's in our history book."

"Mmm."

"Do people know?"

"Know what? That I had a famous great grand uncle?"

"Yes. And that he was born here."

"People nowadays have no interest in such things."

I turned the pages and found some illustrations. I could make little sense of them. Then I found a portrait of the author. I scrutinised him but found no resemblance to Charlie. But then it had taken me a long time to recognise the features of the house in a photograph of it, so maybe he was right, maybe detection was not my strong point.

"How long would it take you to read it?"

"I'd say a long time. It's a book for grown-ups."

"I'll lend it to you for a fortnight, and we'll see how you get on."

"But you said it's never been out of the house before."

"That's right, but I think I can trust you to mind it."

"I would. But are you sure?"

"A fortnight. And then I'll expect you to tell me what's in it."

"I will. I'll be very careful with it."

I could scarcely believe that he was giving me the loan of this book. Breathless, I watched him wrap it carefully in a double sheet of the 'Irish Independent'. He placed it in the bottom of my shopping bag.

"Be careful of the eggs now. If you break one, it will drip all over the book."

In a state of terror I cycled home. Every slight twist of the handlebars sent shivers through me. Every bump of the wheels wrenched the breath out of me. But I was an expert at ferrying home large bagfuls of eggs without breaking any. So when I unpacked the bag I found the book nestling safely at the bottom.

When Mother enquired what I had there, I replied that it was just a book Charlie had lent me. I took it to the front room and lay down on my bed fondling it and smelling the musty leather of the cover. Whenever I opened it I was daunted by text I could not comprehend.

Later I brought it out to the kitchen where Mother and Father were sitting back, as they usually did on a Sunday afternoon, reading the newspaper. I showed them the book and told them about Charlie's famous great grand uncle. Mother fingered through the illustrations and when she came to the portrait, she began picking out the features that resembled Charlie's.

"Where's the book we have?" I asked.

"Do you mean 'The Golden Treasury'?"

There was only one book I could mean.

"It's up there in the press," she said.

I got a chair and climbed up. In among the bags of sugar and the bags of flour, the bextartar, and the tea, I found it. There was no cover on it, back or front, and the first page was numbered xxiv. I wiped off the coating of flour and sugar and crumbs.

"Can I have this?"

"You can if you want it. It's been lying around long enough."

I brought it with me and went back to lie on the bed, examining it. Yes, it had been lying around for long enough. I recalled its having a tattered red cover one time. How long had it been in the family? Maybe a hundred years, like Charlie's book. It was our book, our family heirloom, and now I owned it.

I opened it and began to leaf through the pages. Most of the introduction was missing and the last page ended in the middle of a poem, so there were pages missing there too. However, in between, the book seemed to be intact. Some of the poems were familiar, 'Simon Lee, the Old Huntsman', 'The Poplar Field', and I recalled Mother reading them to us years before in the kitchen in Killenduff.

There were poems that I could not comprehend, others that couldn't have been simpler.

'She dwelt alone and few could know
When Lucy ceased to be
But she is in her grave
And, oh, the difference to me.'

I lay back, the book resting on my chest, wondering who Lucy was and why the poet missed her so much.

17

My faculty of smell has never been strong. It is almost useless, in fact. But a few, probably no more than five, smells have been indelibly pressed on my mind's nose. Even today when I smell Palmolive soap, I immediately recall the bar Mother bought on that first holiday back in Killeenduff. Every morning it was on the side table in the kitchen, beside the tin basin where each of you washed your hands and the sleep from your eyes. Yes, I remember the smell of Palmolive soap and that wakening jab of icy water to the face.

The smell of woodbine, no matter where I have encountered it, always takes me back to the Forge Road, just above the Corner, where the Travellers used to camp. It grew profusely through the hedge there, and every summer its powerful aroma drifted up or down the road, depending on which way the wind blew. Whenever the sea breeze was most assertive the aroma of woodbine followed you and your buckets all the way to Maloney's well.

Now, as I walk the Forge Road, looking for that snug patch of grass under the sycamore trees where the Travellers used to camp, I imagine I can still smell the woodbine, even though it is not the time of year.

And the imagined smell reminds me of that day towards the end of summer when Mother came up here and collected sprigs for the vase she had. You remember that vase. It was the only ornament in the house, probably a wedding present, and what happened you certainly remember. I remember it still, with pain.

She had put the vase of woodbine on the low shelf of the sideboard, and was sitting by the fire, relaxed now that the work was done, teaching Eileen how to knit. The house was tidy and clean, and the sense of peace was overwhelming.

You were sitting spread-eagled on the floor running your rubber handball against the wall under the sideboard. You were so intensely conscious of the peace. And it was the peace that possessed you, filled you with joy, and as the delight in the moment welled up, you threw the ball harder and harder along the floor, quite unconsciously. When the delight overflowed into ecstasy, you threw the ball so hard it bounced off the floor, hitting the vase of woodbine, toppling it. It fell to the cement floor and broke into a thousand pieces. With what dismay you stared at those shards of pottery, the scattered sprigs of woodbine, the patch of water spreading across the cement floor. You were scarcely conscious of Mother's wail, her flailing arms, of Eileen's knitting all tangled in the chaos you had unwittingly caused. You were stunned by the awareness of the extraordinary peace that lay shattered with the shards of vase.

18

"Can I go and make the tea now?"asked Mikey. "Can I go with him?" added Eileen. They were no sooner on the bog than they were tired and bored.

"Alright," I conceded. At least I wouldn't have to listen to their complaining for a while. "Bring down the billy-can to the fire. You'll see a barrel of water there, with a tap on it. Fill the billy-can and put it on the fire. Put it well in, but be careful not to burn yourself, and don't let the others shift your can or you'll be there all day trying to get it boiled. When it starts bubbling take it off, throw in the tea-leaves, and get back here as fast as you can."

I was a veteran at this stage and took pride in, and not a little satisfaction from, dishing out the orders and directions. Father had hesitated when it had come to letting Eileen and Mikey out on the bog, concerned that they were too young, but after a few days of the summer holidays they started agitating.

They complained that everyone else was out on the bog, and there was no one left in The Park to play with. They imagined we were having a carnival out on Trench Three, setting off with a picnic every morning, so they kept pestering Father until he relented. He conceded that they might be some help to me during the day, if only to make the tea. And as soon as Mikey arrived on the bog and saw the great bonfire lit strategically at the bottom of the trench, with safety drains all around it, he was fired with enthusiasm for making the tea.

Father's qualms about having younger children working on the bog were not shared by others, because whole platoons of families were out now. Sometimes I would pass a plot with a woman and perhaps six children of all ages in it, with even the youngest making a contribution. Mother sometimes expressed an interest in coming out, but Father asserted that it would be too much for her on top of her housework.

His scruples had extended to questioning the propriety of having Eileen and Mikey on the bog. I questioned it too, but I soon made up my mind. I needed the company. With the extra forces now deployed, the plots around us were being finished, and we were being left behind. Despite Father's efforts in the evenings, we were painfully slow turning the spread turf into footings. Mikey was able to do a little, so was Eileen, but I was disappointed to find that my own work-rate fell miserably short of what my peers were managing.

Being left behind had other implications too. Now that the main workforce had moved down the bog about half a mile, so had the fire. It took Eileen and Mikey a long time to reach it, and by the time they returned with the billy-can the tea was stone cold. Nevertheless, I was glad to be relieved of that chore, as it was embarrassing to be meeting people I knew and having to cope with their enquiries as to where I was working and how much I had done.

Yes, I was glad of their company. The bog was a curious and eerie place when there was no one around. The silence was terrifying. It was total. There were no birds to sing in this brown desert, no trees to whisper a response to the caressings of the wind. There was no traffic noise. Occasionally I would be re-assured by the sound of a machine in the far distance, or the staccato chugging of a locomotive pulling a row of wagons up the central line that ran between Trench Three and Trench Four as far as the yard.

Days passed, and I was mortified at being left so far behind and was driving myself harder and squeezing as much work as I could out of Eileen and Mikey. I had them working on the bottom end of the plot where the turf was drier and lighter. When we paused to eat now, instead of sitting down to Eileen's carefully laid-out picnic, we ate our sandwiches with urgency and drank cold milk instead of tea. And finally the plot was finished. The rows didn't look too pretty, especially at the bottom, but the turf was footed and we were finished at last.

It was late in the afternoon when we walked self-importantly down along the trench to take our next plot. I was anxious to have a start made on it before Father arrived. It was disconcerting to see how far we had fallen behind, to see how many plots had been turned into dark brown footings. Eventually we arrived where people were working, finishing off plots, then where plots were only half-done, and finally where plots were barely started. There were groups here and there at the butt of the turf clamp taking their afternoon break. The atmosphere was strangely lethargic.

When we passed all the people who were working and all the afternoon tea drinkers, we arrived at the first vacant plot. We placed our coats and bags in a bundle at the base of the clamp and proceeded to put up our few footings to claim the plot. As soon as we had the footings up to stake our claim, all the little huddles of people who had been taking their break down along the clamp started packing up. People quickly came past us to take new plots. There were dozens of them, all urgency, all energy, hurrying past us with their heads down.

I became anxious and suspicious. How could so many of them have finished their old plots simultaneously? I took a walk over the turf in our plot. There was a dip in the middle of the plot, a wet recession, where the rows of turf were pitched on top of one another, and were still soaking wet, almost as they had been left by the bagger. It looked ugly, awful. I then proceeded to walk down the middle of the following plots. My suspicions were justified. They were all dry, and the rows were well spaced, conditions that made the turf easier to foot, a million times easier. My stomach sank, my heart sank, I had been fooled.

I went back, full of anger and indignation, determined to tackle the plot and show them I was not put out by their blackguarding. I put Eileen and Mikey working on the best rows, but even those were wetter and softer than any we had encountered previously. I started on one of the really bad ones, where the sods were pitched so closely together they were stuck to one another. Only a thin rib on the exposed back of each sod was dry. I had to separate the sods before I could put them in a footing and had to take one sod carefully at a time instead of being able to lash them up two at a time.

I had made a little progress down into the plot when we had a visit from the ganger, Christy Morris.

"Christ Jesus," he ground out the words as if he were munching them in anger between his teeth before he spat them out at me, "what do you think you're doing?"

He was standing over me with a long white lath in his hand. I had been so intent on the task that I had not seen him approach. He had a fearsome reputation.

"Do you call that footing?" He stuck his lath into my last construction and tipped it over. "Four sods high is no footing. I want those turf to dry. And they won't dry if they're not twice as high as that."

"But if I put any more turf up, they'll break, Mr. Morris." My voice was trembling just as every other part of my body was trembling.

"Look, I'm paying to get a job done. Now if you can't do it, get to hell out of here. Just look at this." He strode across the spread turf stamping his wellingtons into them as if deliberately reducing them to mush. "What's he doing? Making sand castles?" He took a kick at a little mound of muck that Mikey was putting together from the debris of wet sods. "What's this supposed to be?"

I looked down at the scattered rubble, at the round wet mark on the toe of the ganger's wellington. "Sorry, Mr. Morris. We'll try to do them better." I stuttered out these words, remembering Father's advice not to cross these people.

"Try?" His red face was puffed in petulance. "What do you mean, 'try'? Do you think I owe you a living or something? There's no 'trying' about it. Either you can do the work or you can't, and if you can't, I want you off the bog so fast I won't see your arse for the dust rising after you. Is that understood?"

"Yes, Mr. Morris."

He stormed off down the bog, scarcely glancing at the work in the other plots.

"He's nasty," said Eileen, who was standing white-faced looking at me.

"What will we do?" asked Mikey.

"We'll do them better," I snapped.

"But the sods won't stay together. They fall apart," he tried to explain, standing at the end of the line of rubble that was supposed to be a row of footings.

"Ah, go and make the tea then. If you're no good on the bog you'll have to stay at home."

When Father arrived, he was dismayed.

"Why did you take this plot?" he asked in a wail. "Why didn't you wait for me?"

"I thought we had to take the next plot as soon as we were finished. But I think a lot of them were finished before us, and were hanging back until this plot was taken. As soon as we had started they all came up to take the next plots."

"I bet they did. And I bet they're having a good laugh at us now, the bastards." I was shocked to hear Father swear with venom. "We won't have this plot finished till Christmas," he added, throwing off his coat and starting a row straight away.

Mikey returned with the tea, which was hot because the fire was only a short distance away, but that brought little comfort as we ate in silence.

"And we had a visit from Christy Morris" I threw in after a while. "He was giving out about the footings and said if we can't do them better he'd run us."

Father spat on the ground. "That fellow is nothing but a walking bag of shite. He thinks he can lord it over people just because they made him a ganger. But he'll get what's coming to him one day. When I see him I'll give him a piece of my mind. I'd like to see the effort he'd make at fishing the turf out of this swallow hole."

I was heartened a little by Father's defiance, but that was not enough to dispel the crushed feeling of having failed him.

19

Sometimes I feel like one of those forlorn figures we see on television scraping the ruins of a landscape after an earthquake for fragments of what was.

I walk the road searching for traces of houses you knew, where you were always welcome. Little John's, and I doubt he ever heard of Robin Hood, is gone. There is scarcely a trace of the walls left, certainly no trace of the rich thatch in which he used to hide the hair he trimmed off you and off most of the townland menfolk. He wasn't a barber, just the man who on a whim bought a hair-trimmer in Barton Smiths one fair day in Sligo. I think I knew once why he refused to burn the hair, and insisted on secreting it in the thatch. There was a story there, but I seem to have forgotten it.

The next house, Daisy and Tessie's, is still standing, but deserted since those two old ladies died. I listen for the exotic call of their guinea fowl, but hear only the grumbling rooks who have taken possession of that magical garden. And the briars hold sway over the path, so that I cannot ascertain whether the old grandfather clock still stands inside the front door.

The house of Daniel's Pat is derelict as indeed it almost was while he was still living in it. I often recall the luxurious taste of those skinny bars of Cadbury's chocolate he always had for you when you paid him a visit. You always marvelled at the meticulous way he swept the floors of his upper bedroom and his kitchen, even though there was no roof over them. As the roof fell in on each of them, Pat merely cleared away the heap of mouldy thatch and retreated, until he was finally living in the only room that was still covered.

The house of his brother, Daniel's John, is almost as

derelict. He kept a bull, and, peering over his wall at the rutting cattle, you and Anthony first divined the mystery of procreation.

They are all gone, but for the little fragments of their lives I am uncovering in the shattered landscape and in my mind.

20

The slip was a paved jetty sloping not down into the river, as one would expect, but in the same direction as the flow, ending in a stone wall, as if the builders had abandoned the idea of making it functional. I had never seen a boat near the place, but it was always packed with swimmers. And because the slope was to the south, the slip was a natural sun-trap which encouraged people to dally before and after swimming.

On top of the wall was mounted a diving board, a genuine spring-board, installed by the Swimming Club. Especially when there were girls around, the older boys were forever giving demonstrations of their diving skills. The channel of the river was deepest just outside the slip and that was where the boats plied, and the occasional barge. But boats were few enough and so that stretch of river was almost totally the domain of the swimmers.

The regular swimmers were older than we were, girls as well as boys, so there was plenty of the usual mating banter. They eyed the four of us very suspiciously when we arrived with our towels rolled up under our oxters. When we togged out, they were staring at us.

"Can you lads swim?" asked Tommy Nulty, whom we knew because he was the captain of the local Gaelic Football Minor Team, a position that gave him absolute right to ask any question he wished of us.

"Of course we can," answered Val, his show of confidence seeking to cloak our dubious mastery of the few strokes Art had taught us.

Evening after evening, for several weeks, sometimes with the dusk so thick about us we could scarcely see beyond the banks of reeds that sheltered the sand-beds from a wind perpetually blowing off the lake, we practised our strokes, Art teaching us the way he had been taught. When we were able to leave the tubes aside and swim about ten strokes unaided, we felt we were ready to advance to the river.

"I don't believe you," said Tommy. "I've never seen you down here before. Has anyone seen them down here before?" He turned around and those who were listening to him shook their heads.

"Look lads, it's no place here for bathing. Look at that current. You'd be swept away in a minute. It's dangerous, and I don't want to be searching for you at the bottom of the river, or maybe down past the point."

"It's alright," said Val. "We can swim, honestly. You show them, Art."

Art stepped quickly forward, and dived straight out into the current. He took a few quick strokes downstream then turned and with a surge against the current he swam back to the slip.

Tommy was staring at him open-mouthed. "Yeah, he's good. He's very good. Are the rest of you as good?"

"Naw," said Paddy, "but we can swim a wee bit. Will you keep an eye on us?"

"Alright, but keep close to the bank, and don't go further than the stone there." He pointed out a rock that was jutting above the water about twenty or thirty yards down river. "When you reach that stone, get out and come back. That way you'll be safe enough and we'll be able to keep an eye on you."

"Thanks."

"Where did your man learn to swim?" Tommy addressed the question to Paddy.

"Ah, he learned back in his home place, Erris."

"It must have been the fish that taught him. He's bloody good."

"Ay, isn't he?"

Paddy, Val, and I eased ourselves into the water, pushed off, and paddled our few strokes, making sure to stay within arm's reach of the bank as Tommy had advised us. He stood watching us until he saw that we could in fact swim, and then he went back to his companions.

"He's a decent sort," said Paddy as we pulled ourselves out of the water beside the appointed rock marker.

It was sheer exhilaration to experience that pull of the river, knowing that underneath was twenty foot of rapidly flowing water. Again and again we went back to the slip and swam the short stretch to the rock. The current made it an easy swim - even if we had moved neither arm nor leg we would have been swept that distance anyway, provided we stayed afloat, and each time we moved a little further out into the stream.

From the moment he dived into the water, Art adopted the river, or perhaps the river adopted him. He was like one of those large bream we saw from the bridge sometimes, coming into view out of the depths of the bog-brown water, then disappearing again, to surface yards away. He frolicked in the water, swam like a sprinter, turned over and floated with the stream as if he were letting himself be carried off down past the point and out into the lough. But no matter how strong the current was, Art could turn around and swim against it with greater ease than we enjoyed swimming with it.

When we finally went back to the slip to dry ourselves, Tommy said to Paddy, "Why don't you all come down here on Saturday morning. The Swimming Club has a coach and he'll give you lessons."

"We can't," replied Paddy. "We're all working on the bog."

"What time on Saturday morning?" asked Art.

"About ten o'clock."

Art turned to the three of us. "We could come down here in the morning and then work on in the evening."

"We could give it a try anyway," said Paddy.

"What have you to learn?" Val asked Art. "You can swim like a porpoise. It might be some use to the rest of us."

"I'll come anyway. There are bound to be a few knacks I can pick up."

"Okay. I'm game," said Val. "What about you, Robbie?"

"I don't mind. Yeah, it would be good to be able to swim well."

"Jeeze, it probably means I'll miss The Navy Lark on the radio in the evening," said Val. He was the only one of us who had a radio at home and he listened to it consistently, relaying back to us the jokes he heard on the comedy shows.

"Do we have to pay for the lessons?" I asked Tommy as we were about to depart.

"They're free, compliments of the Swimming Club."

We were down at the slip at ten o'clock on Saturday morning. Along with the four of us were about a dozen others, some older, some younger. The coach arrived and togged out inside his Morris Minor. When he emerged, his enormous belly was the feature that caught my eye first. He was a middle-aged man with an expression and an air about him that suggested detachment. He didn't ask for names, nor seem to notice that the four of us were new to his class. He just lined everybody up and then told the first person to get into the water.

His first routine was leg movements, and he made each of us in turn hold on to the edge of the slip and demonstrate the movements for the breaststroke. He took some time with Paddy, Val, and me, having recognised that our strokes were not exactly cultured. Art he cleared without a comment.

Then he put each of us into the water in turn just outside the slip to demonstrate the full breaststroke. He stood on the edge, above us, and, as we were swimming against the current we remained in the same spot while he shouted instructions and gave demonstrations with his arms. It was great. He was very precise, and as soon as we adapted according to his instructions, there was an immediate improvement in our strokes.

Of course when Art went into the water and started swimming against the current, he was quickly going out of view up towards the bridge. The coach shouted after him to come back, and the rest of the class was laughing at the good of it. Even the coach was smiling.

"What's your name?" he asked, when Art had come back and was moving his arms and legs slowly to stay level with the slip.

"Art. Art McHugh."

"And where did you learn to swim?"

"At home. In Erris."

"You must have practised with the seals."

I could see Art wincing and blushing, not sure, no doubt, whether the comment was derogatory or complimentary.

"Let me see you swim down to the life-belt and back again," said the coach.

Art turned and with powerful graceful strokes he shot down river the couple of hundred yards to where the life-belt stood, just before the point. Then he turned back and faced into the current. With every stroke he buffeted the flowing water and very steadily made his way right back until he arrived at the slip and put his hands on the paving to heave himself up. There was a round of applause from the others.

The coach was standing back, looking at him, admiringly.

"Young man," he said, "you have a natural talent for swimming."

Art blushed. This time there was no ambiguity about the compliment.

Then it was back to the routine of putting the rest of us through our paces. How awkward and ineffective we looked and felt after Art's demonstration.

The coach came over to Art as he dismissed the class.

"If you come every Saturday, I'll give you an extra few minutes at the advanced level," he said. "You could be good."

"What's the coach's name?" I asked a boy called Jim whom I recognised from our school, as we were towelling ourselves dry.

"Eamonn McCarrick. He's good, isn't he? Still wins the top prizes at the galas. Your friend took him by surprise though."

"Yeah, he wasn't expecting that from a beginner."

"You are all in Mrs. Kelly's class in the Fire Station?" he stated rather than asked, referring to the shed across the road from the school that had been commandeered for an additional classroom.

"Yeah, but we're finished now. When we go back we'll be in the main school."

"Over to the Wire Puller," said Jim with an emphasised weariness in his voice.

"Over to who?" I asked, puzzled.

"The Wire Puller, the Master. Have you not heard about him?"

"I've heard of the Master, of course, plenty about him. But why do you call him the Wire Puller?"

"Because he pulls everyone's wire of course. And it's not me that calls him that, it's everyone."

I was speechless, trying to work out the implication of what Jim was saying. But Val's attention had been riveted.

"What do you mean, he pulls everyone's wire?"

"Christ, you don't want a demonstration, do you? He gropes between your legs in class and if he takes a liking to you he keeps you back after school to give your wire a good pulling."

"Jeeze," said Val, "and do people let him?"

Jim gave a dismissive shrug. "When you know the Master better, you'll know that it's not a matter of letting him. You'll be so scared you'll be stiff, including your willie, even if you haven't the horn yet."

We looked at each other blankly.

"Does he do anything to the girls?" asked Paddy.

"No," said Jim, "he's strictly a wire puller."

"Jeeze," said Val. And we finished dressing in silence.

21

The most poignant of all the ruins I have visited since I came back to Tireragh must be the few stones that are left standing of the MacFirbis castle in Lecan. Sheep and cattle graze where once scholars congregated, where the Yellow Book of Lecan was meticulously hand-written, and the Great Book of Lecan and the Book of Genealogies.

For seven hundred years, possibly more, our ancestors, the O'Dowd chieftains of Tireragh, supported and protected the great family enterprise of the MacFirbises. Generation after generation they accumulated the knowledge and the wisdom of the whole country, recording, shaping the dates and the anecdotes into a credible history. They recorded the great Táin Bó Cuailgne, and many more of the legends and myths of Ireland.

Their books grew with the centuries, hoarded for the inspection of visiting scholars, used as a reference in teaching new generations of poets and scribes and historians. The books have survived. After being carried around in knapsacks for hundreds of years, they are now preserved under glass in museums.

Dubhaltach, the last of the dynasty, was removed from Lecan by the Cromwellian planters, at the same time as his patrons were deprived of their lands and banished to the mountains. But Dubhaltach had friends and admirers even among the English, and took refuge in Easkey to finish off his last great work. Ironic that he should fall at the hands of a Cromwellian planter. An old man, he had come to the assistance of a girl who was being molested by the buck, Thomas Crofton. The row took place in a tavern in Farnaharpy, and Dubhaltach's death brought to an end the greatest scholarly dynasty in Gaelic Ireland.

Looking now at the few stones in the field, my mind is mesmerised trying to imagine this place in the days of its glory. One figure from the dynasty particularly fascinates me, Tomⵏs Cam. His nick-name roots him in the everyday world. Cam means 'crooked' but he was unlikely to have been dishonest, more likely a hunchback. I imagine him as a hunchback, anyway, working away on the Great Book, structuring the random data into history. Is the very history of Ireland the creation of Tomⵏs Cam? He certainly had a creative mind and sneaked in stories of his own. Looking north over the Atlantic, was he inspired to pen the story of The Children of Lir? His was the first record of it, so who knows? The story is still in circulation nearly eight hundred years later. It has lasted nearly as long as the formidable exile of Fionnuala and her brothers, as long as that other creation of his family, the history of Ireland.

22

"So that's it finished, then?" asked Eileen incredulously, as I put the final touches to the last footing on the last row. She knew very well it was, but I understood her question. It was in my mind too. It was hard to believe that we were finally shut of it. Eight days we had spent looking at those awful soggy turf and those awful tipsy footings. Had the sun not been shining for the eight days drying up the ground and the turf, it would have taken us longer. Had it been raining, we would have struggled in the plot for the rest of the summer. As it was, Father had done most of the work in the evenings.

Eight days it had taken us, when most individual men would do a plot every day, when most family squads would do far more than a plot in the day. We had been left so far behind that nobody was working within a mile of us, and the fire was so far away we were drinking the cold milk every day instead of hot tea. There was one advantage to being left so far behind. The gangers had moved with the work and for days none of them had been around snooping to see how high the footings were.

We gathered up our bags and coats and began the long trek down the bog to re-join the cohorts who were attacking plot after plot.

"We won't earn as much money as we thought," said Mikey. "Do you think we'd still be able to buy a cow? Daddy said we would buy a cow out of the money we earned, and that he would teach me to milk him."

"Her," corrected Eileen. "A cow is a 'she' not a 'he'."

"I hope we earn enough to go to Sligo at the end of the summer. He told me we would hire Jimmy Leonard's lorry and go down to Killeenduff if we earned enough," I said, not at all confident now that that magical aspiration could be realised.

I nursed my sense of grievance as we eventually spotted white shirts or dresses bobbing in the distance. I was determined never again to be fooled, and mustered my determination as I passed the main body of footers, and approached the plots that had been newly taken.

We were joined in this final part of the trek by Albert Walsh. He had just finished a plot and was on his way to take another. Albert was a couple of years older than me and came from north County Longford. It was unusual to have people living in The Park from so close at hand. Albert was always immaculately dressed, even while working on the bog, but he was also regarded as a phenomenon because he could finish a plot every day by himself just like the best of grown men.

Despite the gap in age, Albert was always friendly towards me and my friends. In fact he was always smiling and polite to everyone. I liked him a lot.

"I hope they're keeping good ones for us up here," he said in his habitual light-hearted manner.

"They'd better be," said I, "because I'm not going into one like the last."

"That was a bloody awful plot you were in. It must have been the worst plot on this side of the trench. Are you finished only now?"

"Yeah, we've been in it for eight days, with Christy on our backs into the bargain."

"The worst plot in the bog and Christy on your back – you deserve a break. We'll have a good look at what's up here, and if they aren't good, we won't go rushing into them."

When we reached the first vacant plot, Albert and I walked over and back across it, then up and down. It was dry, and a thousand times better than the plot we had finished, but yet it wasn't good. There was an area in the centre of it where ten or fifteen rows of turf had been pitched too closely together. Albert pointed out that these rows would be difficult to manage because the sods would have to be separated from one another before they could be put up into footings. They were dry, so they wouldn't crumble, but one would lose a lot of time trying to prise them apart. We stepped through the succeeding plots and they were without blemish.

"What do you think of the first plot?" I asked Albert.

"It's not great. The way I look on it, someone has to do it, but it doesn't have to be us." He laughed his merry mischievous laugh. "Come on," said he.

He led the way to the clamp, and quickly clambered over it. I stood back to let Eileen and Mikey follow him. On the other side of the clamp was a peaceful no-man's-land. Across from us, about fifty yards away, was the clamp belonging to Trench Two, but in between were the few remnants of original bog, patches of gorse, heather, little pools of marsh.

"This is the ideal place for a rest after your hard work on that plot. What do you think?" said Albert with his wry smile.

"Yeah, and I'm dying for a mug of tea. We haven't had a drop of bog tea for days."

Eileen and Mikey got out the billy can. They took Albert's can as well and headed off in the direction of the fire.

"Now, we'll sit tight and see what happens," said Albert.

We sat back comfortably on the seats we had made ourselves from flat dry sods, and looked vacantly at the clouds. The surreptitious indolence was delicious.

After a little while enjoying the silence and the relaxation of our muscles, I asked Albert a question I had been keen to ask for some time. "How do you foot so fast."

Albert thought for a minute or two, as if he were trying to work it out. "I don't know rightly. I suppose it comes natural to me. The most important thing is rhythm, to create a rhythm and to hold it. I saw you working and you were lifting each sod and putting it on top of the footing, straightening your back every time. That's severe on the back and a waste of energy. You have to think of yourself as a machine, with rows in front of you, not sods. Watch."

He got up and spread some of the dry turf from the clamp

out on the ground as if they were ready to be footed. He then bent down in front of them. "This is the way I do it. I keep my back in the one position and let my arms do the work. And let the rhythm take over, turning the sods, catching them with my hands, flicking them on to the footing." I marvelled at the way his hands and arms moved rhythmically, so that one action ran into another flawlessly, several actions becoming a single movement.

I went over to his sods and laid them out again to have a go. He put his hand on my nape and shoved my head down until it was almost touching the turf. "Now, lift your backside, and spread your legs. That's the way." I copied his method, and although my movements lacked the ease of Albert's, I felt that I had been given a very useful lesson.

"It's better to work up the hill, because you have a shorter distance to stretch for the sods," he added as we returned to our seats at the base of the clamp. "And I find it helpful to be humming a song or a tune in my head to keep the rhythm going. What's your favourite song?"

"The Rocks of Bawn."

He threw his eyes up to heaven. "No, that's too slow. You won't get up to a plot a day humming that one. Think of a faster one, a jazzier one, and imagine you are out on a dance floor with some beautiful bird. That will keep you moving, and keep your mind off the drudgery as well."

"Yeah," I agreed. "The monotony gets to me. And when my mind wanders, I start thinking of Sligo, so that all I want to do is lie down and day-dream."

"No, that won't get the turf footed! Pick a tune, think of the dance floor, and keep the rhythm going."

"I'll try."

Eileen and Mikey returned with the two billy-cans full of steaming tea. We all sat down and took out the spread of sandwiches to eat.

After a while we heard the rustle of dry turf in the turfclamp. About twenty yards below us a young man came clambering over. When he saw us he flushed and flustered a little, but didn't greet or acknowledge us. He opened his bag, took out a sandwich, and started gnawing it with determination as if he had come across for that sole purpose.

Albert got up leisurely and had a look over the clamp casually. Then he winked at us, and sat down again.

"Nothing moving so far," he whispered.

After that we took turns, Albert and I, to get up and stretch ourselves and scratch our backs, and take a furtive look at that first plot that was still sitting there challenging the world with its vacancy. People were obviously watching from a distance. If other people had come up along the turf bank, like us, they had veered off to make an urgent can of tea, or had decided to take an early evening off in the hope that it would be gone by morning.

Eventually I spotted a woman coming up along the bottom of the bank. She had three small children in tow. I recognised her as a widow from the parish, who cleaned the school during the year to earn her living. Maybe she would take it. I sat down again, saying nothing, staring at the ground, my stomach tight from the suspense.

There was a marshy piece of ground just beyond my feet, with little red flowers growing in it. They were unusual. At least I had never noticed them before. I might not have noticed them then either, had I not been trying to take my mind off the widow, Mrs. O'Byrne was her name I now remembered, coming up towards the plot, looking over it as we had done. I hoped, I prayed she would have the sense not to take it.

"Sundew they call it," said Albert.

"What?"

"The flower," he nodded at the little red knob that I had picked up almost unconsciously, and was studying with the intensity of a botanist.

"Oh."

"It eats flies."

"You're joking."

"I'm not. It's true. It eats flies. Look."

He broke off a twig of heather and stripped it down until there was only a tiny green bud left on the top. He then bent

96

over the cluster of red flowers and touched one of them ever so teasingly with the tip of the heather. Immediately the petals began to rise and to curl across on the moist centre of the flower.

"See, it thinks it has caught a fly."

It was like a nightmare in miniature, the petals, like tentacles, rising and circling the unfortunate victim stuck to the sweet sticky bait in the centre.

"There's one that's closed," said Albert. "It must have caught a fly."

"What does it do when it's finished? Just open up and start all over again?"

"I suppose so. I never looked at one long enough. But if that plot isn't taken soon, this might be our chance to find out."

The young man twenty yards away began getting restless. He put on an elaborate show of packing his bag and folding up his coat slowly as if it had cost him a fortune and he didn't want to crease it, all the time casting surreptitious glances across the clamp. Then he clambered over. Albert and I looked at one another. He winked. We stood up and surveyed the plots. Yes, the widow had taken the bad plot. The young man threw down his bag and coat unceremoniously and started into the second plot.

"Come on," said Albert.

The two of us were over the clamp like a shot.

"You can have the first one," said Albert. "It's the best one around, and you deserve it after what you've been through."

I started footing the first row, my heart pounding in terror that someone would come and dispossess me before I had properly staked my claim. When I glanced over my shoulder I saw people rising, rising from the trench, rising from along the base of the clamp, rising everywhere, coming to grab the good plots. But we were there before them.

After a while Albert came across to me, and we paced the two plots admiring how dry they were, how evenly spread, how level the ground was.

"If you are after coming out of the worst plot on the bog,

you are after walking into the best one," he said. "And remember what I told you about rhythm." And he walked off whistling 'The Yellow Rose of Texas'.

I watched him go to the bottom of his plot. But I continued to put up footings at the top, partly to emphasise my possession, partly to let Albert make some headway before I started at the bottom. I had no desire to start measuring myself against him. But after a while I left Mikey and Eileen working at the top on the row I had started.

"This is an awful lot better," said Mikey. "Isn't it?"

"It is," I agreed, casting an anxious and guilty look down at the plot where Mrs. O'Byrne was working, her head down, her three children piling turf in their rows behind her, their heads barely visible above their finished footings.

"Daddy will be pleased," continued Mikey. "We might catch up now and earn the money for the cow."

"We might save enough for the holiday in Sligo," Eileen was emphatic.

"We might," I agreed, "do all these things. But we still have to work hard."

By now Albert had moved well up into his plot and I walked down across the turf to start at the bottom like him. Yes, Father would be pleased. This new plot was the best on the bog. He might break the long moody silence that engulfed him since the evening he saw us up to our shoulders in the muck of that other plot. But I could enjoy no satisfaction. When I glanced down at Mrs. O'Byrne there was a weight in the pit of my stomach, a weight that I wanted to disgorge, but couldn't.

23

I see from the deeds of the house that I have also regained turbary rights on the mountain and grazing rights on the Cimin. Still I will hardly cut my own turf, much less buy a cow to draw my own milk. And yet I am warmed by the story of the local bishop who, when he was summoned to Rome for the First Vatican Council, insisted on bringing his own cow with him. Was this an act of domestic economy, or did he think the milk in Italy would not sustain him? Perhaps he needed the spiritual sustenance of his own Sligo milk.

Having a link to the Cimin gratifies me though. I recall how you and Anthony would drive your two cows down the Wrack Road in the morning, and drive them back up the hill in the evening. The same road was little more than a dirt track then. It was roughly and intermittently paved with large stones, but the cows followed a meandering path of packed clay, soft under the feet, and you followed the cows, your eyes on the ground to avoid the occasional slops of fresh dung. But, when time allowed, you and Anthony galloped across the Cimin, that headland of commonage jutting towards Donegal, chasing the sheep, high-jumping the siogans, those low walls on which the slatamaras were dried, diving into the bunkers of fine sand.

And I recall too how Uncle Owen used to bring you on the bar of his bike down around the sea road past the old castle and the pier. He would count the sheep in the sea field he had, then back on the bike, past the kiln where the farmers burned their lime, over as far as the Alt. What pleasure he would take from your open-mouthed awe, watching the waves thundering against the sheer face of that cliff. Owen, who died. He wasn't the last to die of Father's doomed family, but he was the closest to Father, and his death the hardest to take. And when Mother brought you on the bus to see him before he died in Sligo Hospital, you saw a town and street lamps for the first time. But what most impressed you were the ghostly faces that emerged out of the winter blackness every time the bus stopped on the way back, and approached the window beside Mother's face. The eternal question that was asked, how is Owen, the eternal answer, not good. And those ghostly faces would show pain and disappointment. He had not brought them on the bar of his bike to see the waves thundering against the Alt, but he had delighted them on sunny Sundays with displays of stylish football-playing. They had crowded on to buses themselves many times to cheer him from the side-lines of football pitches in far-flung places, as he and Father and their other brothers brought glory to the parish, to the county, the only glory worth the sweat.

24

The potatoes were falling in clusters of golden bulbs when I shook them from the stems. We had planted Records in the back garden. Father held that that variety was best for the early crop. But we preferred Kerr Pinks and it was Pinks alone we had planted in the Shan's field. I could see he was right about the Records though, and every time I sank the spade into the ground and unearthed the spread of roots beneath another stalk I left enough of the glowing tubers on top of the ridge to provide a dinner for several people. We had been drawing from this crop since it ripened in the summer and I was now digging about two thirds of the way down the garden.

It was an easy task, and I was in no hurry. The hurly burly of the summer was over, and it had been a good summer. There was very little to be done now on the crops of potatoes and vegetables, and cabbage, other than to watch them mature in the mellow sunlight. I was enjoying the fresh smell of the stalks and of the newly turned clay. The dreamy atmosphere had not dissipated since we returned from our holiday in Sligo and was being nursed by this extended spell of sunny weather.

It was Saturday, and on Saturday we had our dinner in the middle of the day when Father got home from work. It was almost noon when Mother had come into the room to rouse me, at the same time opening the window to let the fresh air make its way around the house still heavy with the odour of sleeping bodies. Only Mikey had been out of bed, excited because in the afternoon Father was taking him to visit a local farmer who had a cow for sale. We were going to buy a cow from the money we had earned on the bog, and Mikey had beseeched Father and Mother to let him be in charge of the cow. Jim the Shan had offered grazing and a small shed in which we could stable her over the winter, for a little fee of course.

It took me only a few minutes to fill the big pot with spuds. With a little time to laze, I went over to sit on the wire fence and continue my day-dreaming of Sligo. The fence consisted of four strands of wire running through concrete posts. Already the wires were stretched and sagging from children swinging on them and sitting on them in daily congregations.

Our garden being first in the row had one fence bordering the lane that ran alongside it. On the other side of the lane, perpendicular to it, were the gardens and back gates of the terrace of two-storey houses. I was swinging gently on the wire, examining a flower I had picked from the rough earth margin outside the fence, when I was surprised to see someone coming out the back door of Molloys' house, surprised because the Molloys were one of the few families who had moved on again leaving their houses vacant.

It was a girl. She was lugging a metal dust-bin and came down through the garden with it, and out the back gate. The bins were collected from the back gates of those houses. She was wearing a blue polka-dot apron over her dress, and she had a light scarf pulled across her head and fixed at the back under her hair, the way some women wore scarves when they were dusting or painting.

When she plonked down the dust-bin, she looked about, and was ever so slightly startled to see me sitting there so close to her. She smiled.

"Hello," I said, articulating the two syllables with great difficulty.

"Hi," she returned the greeting, still smiling warmly as she bolted her back gate.

I watched her return to the house, and then I started to breathe again. She was certainly the most beautiful girl I had ever seen. Underneath the scarf I could see her blond hair falling to her shoulders.

I could not take my eyes off the back door through which she disappeared until my mother's voice broke the spell.

"Robbie, have you the potatoes dug?"

I then remembered where I was and what I was supposed to be about, grabbed the pot of potatoes, hurried into the scullery, threw them in the sink, and ran the cold tap on them. When I had scoured the pot I began scrubbing the potatoes clean of the wads of clay stuck to them, then returning them to the pot, the biggest ones first, ready for boiling.

Mother came out to the scullery with the long sharp knife. "Will you cut a head of cabbage for me, and we'll get the dinner under way?" She took away the pot of spuds, and I happily returned to the garden, brandishing the knife as if I were intent on murder. I took my time selecting a head to cut, glancing every second over towards the girl's back door, but she did not re-appear. The words of that poem from the Golden Treasury came into my head and I kept repeating them to myself over and over, as I perused the rows of cabbage:

> A violet by a mossy stone
> Half hidden from the eye
> Fair as a star when only one
> Is shining in the sky.

I found it curious that I had not heard of the arrival of another family in The Park. Usually a man was working for the Turf Company a while before he moved his family into one of the houses, and Father would have news of such an event long before it happened.

When we were sitting down to dinner I waited for an opportunity of sounding out Father on the subject of the newcomers. It was difficult to get a casual word in edgeways, the way I wanted, with Mikey talking excitedly about the cow, and the afternoon's visit to the farmer, asking questions about milking, scheduling how often he would go out to check on her, setting down his boundaries for fear I might encroach on his territory.

At last there was a lull.

"New people have moved into Molloys' house," I said.

Mikey's face was as alert as a game-cock's when I opened

my mouth, but, as soon as he realised I was not offering any statement on the subject of the cow, he relaxed and addressed himself to the task of eating his dinner in the shortest possible time.

"Really?" said Mother. "I hadn't noticed."

"George Martin is moving into that house," said Father, scooping the last of his bacon broth and bits of cabbage on to his spoon. "He's working down the bog for the last few weeks, and the way things are going, he'd be well advised to get out, instead of tying himself down with a house."

"Why is that?" asked Mother.

"It's all over the bog that Willie Morahan was bragging he would show that black Protestant who had the upper hand now. Poor George seems to be as quiet and polite a man as you would meet in a day's walk. But Morahan was giving off that they had us down for eight hundred years, and by Christ he would teach this so-and-so who was down now. Apparently, it was Christy who took George on, but Willie ordered that he be sent down to the new bog they were opening for Trench Seven, digging drains on piece rate."

"Well, I suppose one job is as bad as the next, but it's not fair to go picking on him just because he's a Protestant," said Mother.

Father shook his head with a rueful smile. "One job isn't as bad as the next. This one stands out on its own. That's why it was such a big joke with the men. Digging a drain in a new bog is almost impossible. If you're employed on time rate you don't care if the drain you have dug has closed in before you leave the bog in the evening. But if you're on piece-rate you have to get it measured by a ganger before it goes into the books for payment. It has to be so deep, and so wide. Now, if the ganger doesn't turn up to measure it until the following day, there might be no more trace of your drain than a scrape on the surface of the bog. Do you see what I'm getting at? I'm sure that Willie Morahan, or any of the rest of them, won't be breaking their necks going down to measure George

Martin's drains as soon as he has them dug. I'll tell you this, I wouldn't like to be facing into the winter he's looking at."

"That's awful," declared Mother in a genuinely shocked voice. "That's awful."

"It's said that they always look after their own. So I hope there's someone somewhere to look after George Martin before the year is out."

And as I sat listening in horror to what was being perpetrated on George Martin, I was terrified for the girl with the scarf around her hair, 'a violet by a mossy stone, half hidden from the eye'.

"And has he a family?" I managed to ask as nonchalantly as I could out of the turmoil in my brain.

"Lucky enough he has just the one daughter, so I suppose he won't need as much as the rest of us to keep going."

"Hazel is her name," piped in Eileen.

"How do you know?" I turned on her too spontaneously, and she eyed me with surprise and curiosity.

"Ann O'Donnell was talking to her down at the shops. She's going to be in Ann's class in school."

My heart soared, plummeted, soared. If they treated her father so badly on the bog, he was unlikely to stay. On the other hand, Ann O'Donnell was Paddy's sister and one of Eileen's best friends, so there might be a chance of seeing Hazel up our end of The Park if she were palling around with Ann and Eileen.

In school she would be in the Fire Station, as Ann was in the class behind Paddy and me, and Eileen was in the class behind that again. Hazel, what a lovely name. 'Fair as a star when only one is shining in the sky.'

"Right, we'd better be off," said Father.

Mikey hopped up too. "And we're going to call him Pruggy," he announced.

"Her," I reminded him.

"Ah, what does it matter?" he shrugged.

Mother laughed. "It matters a lot. If you come back with a 'him', we won't have much milk for the winter."

105

25

I am constantly being startled by little features of the house that twig memories. The nail on which the paraffin lamp was hung is still in the wall coated in layers of paint. Even when the electricity poles came marching down the road, and buzzing men strung a wire across to the house to give three electric bulbs, one suspended from the ceiling of each room, the lamp remained in place, just in case. Some neighbours thought the electricity was a fad which would never catch on and kept absolute faith with the paraffin lamp.

And when you returned on those fortnights in August, there was no power in the house, so you all blissfully gathered at night in the dim light of the paraffin lamp. I must search the antique shops. Nothing else must decorate that nail now.

And the little lip on the front doorstep is still there, the one you tripped on that winter of the great snow. You were chasing the seagulls that were swooping down on the crusts of bread Mother had thrown out for them. You were enjoying tantalising them, running out the door when they approached, back in when they had taken flight. Finally, you slipped or tripped on the doorstep, and smashed your mouth on the ground. I still have the scar on my lip.

26

There was silence in the classroom, the special kind of silence that reigns when examinations are in progress. We were being tested in Irish, English, and Arithmetic, to see who would get into the Scholarship Class. The Scholarship Class would get extra tuition on three days a week and be groomed for the County Council Scholarship examinations at Easter. There was huge prestige associated with those scholarships. Only ten were awarded in the whole county, so anyone who got one was spoken of with respect bordering on awe. That attracted me as much as the financial promise of having my whole secondary education paid for.

We were crammed into the long benches, boys in one row, girls in the next. The Master was moving around as we worked, looking over what each pupil was writing. No one dared look up. We were more than impressed by the jockey's stick he used for a cane with its knob of metal for a handle and its hint of steel at the tip.

I wasn't tempted to look around anyway, absorbed as I was in the test, distracted only by the occasional thought of Hazel over in the Fire Station. Even those lapses of concentration turned rapidly to more intensely inspired efforts as I reflected on the opportunity I now had of enhancing my image in Hazel's eyes. I excelled at nothing clse, absolutely nothing, but this I could do. Without effort I could top the class. Now, if I really tried, I was sure that I could top the county.

Lost in reverie and concentration I had not noticed the Master moving along the row until he was sitting on the bench right in front of me. He flicked around the piece of paper on which I was writing and began to read it. As he was doing so, he ran his hand down between me and the bench, stroking my stomach, moving downwards until his fingers were massaging my groin. So this was it, he was a wire puller as the boy at swimming had put it.

I moved my chest in slowly and steadily until I was squeezing his arm with considerable pressure between me and the edge of the wooden bench. I kept the pressure on as he tried to withdraw his hand and was delighted to feel him writhe in pain as he finally extricated it. I thought for a moment he either was easy to hurt or was exaggerating his pain, as he returned to his duties at the top of the room. But then I noticed him trying to remove a splinter he had acquired from the rough wooden bench. He spread out the first aid kit on his bench and was busy with tweezers and cotton wool and TCP, while I tried to focus again on the test, until he finally called time.

The smell of TCP was all over the classroom as we folded our answer papers and passed them along to the ends of the rows. He put us reading our English books while he marked the tests. Even though we read the assigned story in a few minutes we nevertheless observed a rigid silence. The smell of disinfectant suggested the prudence of not provoking a wounded lion. Finally he tapped his stick twice on the desk, and we obediently looked up at him.

"There are four people in the class who might have a chance of winning a scholarship, as far as I can see from these tests. I want them to stay back after school this evening until we make arrangements for the extra classes." And he started calling out the names slowly, three girls, then mine.

No one blinked at each of the girls' names, but when mine was called, it seemed as if every head in the room swivelled around.

"Jeeze," I heard Val breathe beside me.

It was now three o'clock and the Master rang the hand-bell to dismiss the school. I noticed people looking at me. Paddy was smirking with a sympathetic sort of grin.

"Is he picking on you, or did you really try?" asked Val.

"Of course I tried. Didn't you?"

108

"Are you mad? Try to be kept back after school with that fellow? Do you think I need my head examined?"

"Never mind," said Paddy, still amused, "he'll give you plenty of private tuition, and you'll get a scholarship, no bother."

But I was not amused. I was in cold dread, sick at my own stupidity. I could hardly speak, but managed to tell Paddy to call in and explain to my mother that I would be late home. When he was gone, I regretted having done that: as soon as she heard the news she would be lighting candles of exultation, putting paid to any option I had of dropping out of the class before anyone knew I was selected for it.

The school quickly cleared but for the four scholars sitting rigidly waiting for the Master to finish totting the rolls. Eventually he closed the leather-bound book, gathered the handful of answer papers and made his way down to us.

He sat up on the bench in front of us and began to rummage through the papers.

"The four of you have done well," he said, then added in an absent-minded sort of way, as if we weren't meant to hear, "promising, very promising."

He gave a deep sigh, still examining the papers slowly, as if he had all the time in the world. I glanced at his hand to see if the splinter had made any impression, but could see none.

"Scholarship Class will take place from three to half-past three every Monday, Tuesday, and Wednesday."

I wondered if there was any way I could be unavailable on those days. That would be a convenient escape – if I had chores to do at home. But there wasn't a hope. Father would move mountains, walk through fire, to give me the chance of a good education. He talked of schools and schooling for all of us non-stop. It was our only opportunity of succeeding in life. And he was gratified by my little academic successes: they compensated for the recognition that I would never play football for the county as he had done, nor even for the parish. And I was happy to have him so gratified. Being selected to be tutored specially for a County Council

Scholarship would be the best accolade to date. He would be immeasurably proud. So no, there would be no chance of making the chores a reason for not showing. I was trapped. I had missed the obvious chance of avoiding this predicament, obvious to everyone but me. I was the one lacking intelligence.

The Master continued leafing through the papers slowly. Then he called out one of the girls' names and started making remarks about her answers. When he had done, he handed her answer papers to her, "Now you can go."

She packed her papers into her bag and left. He called out another name, followed the same procedure. And she left. The third name was the last of the girls, and I began to sweat, around the collar of my shirt, under my armpits, down my back. I did not take in a word of what he said about this girl's work, just waited until I saw her too packing her bag.

It was now down to the Master and me. He seemed to loom larger in stature where he was sitting on the bench, and I felt myself dwindle until we seemed a giant and a dwarf.

He started talking about my answers, how good they were, how much promise they showed, and I suddenly realised that he was bullshitting, that he cared nothing about my prospect of winning a scholarship, and the spell was gone. He was no longer a giant, no longer the Master who had power over me, to whom I owed respect and allegiance. He was a wire puller and I was in an awkward corner, but my dread was gone.

He put down my papers on the bench and looked at me with his cold impenetrable smile.

"You're the lucky one," he said. "Back after school with three girls. Does that excite you? Do you like them?"

I looked at him squarely. "They're very nice," I said as if I were answering a question he had asked me in Arithmetic.

He looked out the window. "Ah, I see Mrs. O'Byrne is finished," he said in a wistful tone. I glanced out as well. Sure enough, there was Mrs. O'Byrne leaving the school gate, on

110

her crouched shoulders the weight of the world, making her way across to the Fire Station to complete her work. He had obviously been waiting for this.

"She will have given the toilets a thorough washing down," he went on in a cajoling sort of tone. "What do you say to the two of us going down and splashing all over them."

"No, I wouldn't like to ruin Mrs. O'Byrne's work," I answered in the coldest strongest tone I could muster. Then I sat back, staring at him, as much as to say, 'Right, next question, Wire Puller'.

He was at a loss. He flustered, took up my papers again, made some comments which I didn't hear because I was too intent on cold concentration. Then I did hear him dismiss me with the words, "That will be all. Class will start on Monday."

I bundled up my belongings and left without a word. I was free, at least for now.

Around the corner in The Park, Val and Paddy were waiting for me.

"Well, what happened?" asked Paddy, highly amused at my plight.

I threw my bag on the ground and the three of us sat down under the wall. I told them all that had happened. They had been expecting something more lurid. The anti-climax brought them all down to a more commonplace state of mind.

"I have to get out of this," I said.

"It won't be easy," replied Paddy. "When I told your mother where you were she was dancing a jig with delight."

I groaned. I had no difficulty imagining that scene. And that was nothing to how Father would react when he heard I had been selected for the Scholarship Class.

27

I visited the Rosan today, walked up past Flannelly's house, and on to where the footbridge crossed the Easkey River. Every autumn the hazel wood that spread up from the bank of the river was heavy and golden with clusters of nuts.

It was one of those images that haunted you as you lay awake in the front room in Ballyclare, clutching the Golden Treasury, reading the titles of the poems with the help of the dim street light, imagining poems about the Rosan. When the girl, Hazel, ignited your mind, you matched her immediately to this location, and began to toss words together, forcing them to rhyme, to tie the lines to one another as you so desperately wanted to tie Hazel to this landscape, and to you.

The river still flows with its old, relentless, though leisurely pace. Often you and Anthony came here, staring into the pools at the brown trout that were always too nimble for your gauche attempts at snatching them. And you plotted to employ more effective though brutal strategies, resolving to listen more attentively when adults were recounting their successes in blowing up the river with bottles of quicklime. It was illegal to fish the river, as the rights had been left in the possession of the landlords even after the lands on either bank from source to mouth had been confiscated. They had their bailiffs still patrolling the river on the watch for poachers. And you all wanted to be poachers, and have tales to tell of thwarting the bailiffs. You all wanted to tilt at this last relic of landlordism.

28

It was unusual for people to visit at our house in The Park. Back in Sligo the door was always open and people came rambling in at every time of the day and night. Here, because we were all strangers to one another, because we were now living in a town, there was a distance between neighbours despite the far greater proximity of their houses.

A ripple of surprise and anticipation ran through the family therefore when Tom Brennan and Donal Fitzgerald called at the door asking for Father. Mother went out and invited them in. I was sitting at the kitchen table doing my school homework. Frank and Billy were told immediately that it was their bedtime. Mother asked Eileen and Mikey to come and help her wash the dishes in the scullery out the back. That left the kitchen reasonably empty and Father invited the two men to sit on the couch, while he pulled up a kitchen chair to sit opposite them. I kept my head in my books in the hope that I wouldn't be disturbed.

"We're thinking of organising the Union in the job," said Tom Brennan to Father, "and we were wondering whether you would join."

"Well, I suppose if everyone else is joining I'll join," said Father with a significant lack of enthusiasm.

I pretended to concentrate on my homework even though I found the opening of this conversation quite diverting. I understood immediately Father's dilemma. Frequently I heard him rail about Tom Brennan and other fitters and turners who were paid the full rate but did less work than he did. Tom, who was Val's father, being a city man, had the air of being knowledgeable and self-confident and that didnot endear him to his workmates who came from the remote untamed quarters of the country. However, I encountered him regularly when I called on Val, and found him to be very friendly and pleasant in manner.

"We may not get everyone," said Donal. "You know yourself the situation in the Company. But we'll get the majority to start with, and we'll get the rest of them later."

"It will be a struggle to get the Union started, and to get recognition," continued Tom. "But we have been getting advice from the local organiser of the Workers' Union. Once even a few of us join, he will guarantee the support of the Union. Then, what we need is an issue or a couple of issues. That's why we came especially to you, Joe. We would like to make an issue of your rate. Everyone agrees it is a total injustice that you are not getting the tradesman's rate when you are fully qualified and doing the work. It will be the perfect case to hit the management with."

"Oh, I don't know," said Father. "They say they're hoping to sort it out for me soon. They say it's the crowd in Head Office that are holding it up."

"It's going on a long time now," said Tom, "and there's no sign of them to deliver. Blacksmiths are employed on other bogs, and they are paid the full rate, so I doubt that Head Office is the problem. I think the local bods are the problem. Who's supposed to be following it up?"

"Well, I talk to Willie Morahan about it regularly. He says he talks to the Manager."

There was a spontaneous reaction of contempt from the two men at the mention of Willie Morahan.

"Morahan is stringing you along," declared Donal. "He will do nothing for any man unless it's a dirty deed. The man takes delight in making other people suffer."

"Ah, that's not fair," said Father jumping to the defence of his fellow countyman.

"The man is a bully and a blackguard of the lowest order, Joe. You know that and everyone knows it. He's probably doing nothing about your rate and taking pleasure in the grief it's giving you. We need the Union to nail the bully boys like Morahan." Tom was practically stamping on the floor in indignation.

114

"What do you mean, nail him?" asked Father in some alarm.

"Nail him. Get rid of him."

"But he's not all that bad."

"He is too," chipped in Donal. "Do you know that he has squeezed money out of nearly every man on the bog, money he borrows, but never repays? That's extortion. He's a single man with no family responsibilities. The men he leans on are living from hand to mouth, and with plenty of mouths to feed at that. But how can any man refuse him money when he knows that might mean the losing of his job. And losing the job for most would mean losing the house as well."

"I never heard he was taking money." Father sounded surprised, shocked.

"Well, he is, and worse. You heard how he has George Martin digging drains at piece-rate down on the fresh bog."

"I heard that, and I agree, that's not right."

"If we make an issue of George's situation, we will get every labourer on the bog into the Union. And if we can make an issue of your case, we will get the men in the Workshop behind us. Two straightforward issues are all we need, and if we make them back down on those issues, we will have established the Union. Then they will have to sit down and talk with us about a hundred other problems." Tom was emphatic.

"And what makes you think they'll back down?" Father sounded doubtful.

"Because if they don't, they'll have a strike on their hands."

"Strike?" Father sounded like a man who had been hit by a mallet.

"It'll probably come down to that, Joe," Donal chipped in. "You know what they're like. They're unlikely to listen to reason. But we'll try. We'll ask them to negotiate. But I think we all know how the Manager will react to that. So we have to be prepared to go out."

"I don't know. I'd have a problem about Willie Morahan.

115

You know he comes from the same county as myself."

"I know that. But Morahan is no credit to any county. Do you know how much George Martin had in his pay packet last week when the rent of the house was taken out? Ten shillings! How is a man supposed to support a family on ten shillings?"

"That's blackguarding alright," agreed Father strongly. "I wouldn't stand over that. George is a quiet inoffensive man. He shouldn't be treated like that."

"Well there's many a man down the bog getting a raw deal, and Morahan is at the root of most of it. Ten shillings! You wouldn't offer it to a gasun for making the tea." Donal was from the south of Ireland, and the children were fond of imitating his musical accent. Every Sunday afternoon he went up on the playing field with a bunch of make-shift hurleys under his arm, teaching the young boys to play hurling, a game that was foreign to the Midlands, and indeed to many of the western and northern counties the rest of us came from.

"What do you say, Joe?" asked Tom.

"I'll think about it. I'll join the Union alright, but bringing the men out on strike is a serious matter. They could leave us out till we starved. They could dump us out of the houses. Nearly every man has a family to look after. I have six kids to think about, and another one on the way."

"We all have families to think of and if we decide to go out, it's going to be rough. But we have to be determined to win. If we pick our time, and if we stick together, there isn't much they can do. They have to get their turf cut. And at the end of the day I can't see the Manager, or Head Office for that matter, putting a year's production at risk for the sake of the few quid they're holding from you. And as far as Morahan is concerned, when his blackguarding is seen to have caused a strike, they're not going to stand behind him. Oh, no, they'll hang him out to dry." Tom was so sure of everything, he amazed me.

"Okay," said Father. "I'll think about it."

"Great," said Donal, "but don't leave it too long. We need

to be organised and ready to hit them in the spring, just before the baggers go out."

"I do appreciate what you're doing," said Father. "But it's a serious step and I don't want to get chucked out on the side of the road. Neither do I want to be packed off to Carndonagh or Bangor Erris. I like it here. It's a good town. They have schools for the kids, and plenty of jobs. This is where I want to bring up my family."

Donal nodded. "We all do, Joe. We're all planning on staying. That's why we have to get things sorted out. This will be a great place, and working for the Company will be a great job if we don't have the likes of Morahan walking all over us."

They rose to go. Father suddenly remembered the ritual of hospitality and invited them to stay for a cup of tea. But they declined. They had just eaten dinner, like ourselves, and wanted to fit in another call before it was too late to visit people.

I kept my head buried in my books and the men left without acknowledging my presence. I was thrilled and awed. What they were proposing seemed momentous. It left me gasping. And the linking of Father and George Martin was exciting for other reasons. I could think of myself and Hazel linked as a result.

Father didn't seem to note my presence either, and when he came back in from the door he sat down as if he were in a daze.

Mikey and Eileen came skipping in. "What did they want, Daddy? What did they want?"

"Nothing," said Father, as if his mind were far away. "Nothing at all."

29

It was those holiday trips back to Killeenduff that kept your heart from breaking. Is that an overstatement? Perhaps not. Hearts do not physically break, and the human being has enormous resilience, an enormous capacity to survive, to adapt to changed circumstances, to grow into new environments, but the soul of a child can be crushed like a beetle under a hob-nailed boot. Aboard Jimmy Leonard's lorry, careering over the Curlews, you were always miles ahead of the hob-nailed boot.

It was a returning of a kind. All the furniture on the back of the lorry, just as it had been when you went in the opposite direction. All the children in the nest inside, where Mother led the sing-song. And you made sure to be on the back of the lorry this time. Sitting on folded bed-clothes between the four legs of the up-turned kitchen table, you croaked out the songs with as much gusto as if you were performing on 'Ballad Makers, Saturday Night'.

What big cheers you all gave when you passed the sign, 'Co Sligo', the old forge near Riverstown where Father had served his time. Jimmy even beeped the horn, no doubt to salute Father's former employer. Then after the bridge in Ballisodare you all went quiet. You were in Tireragh. There was no need of songs now to fan you to ecstasy. All were looking through the rungs to catch the first glimpse of the sea, the first glimpse of Ballykillcash Tower. And when you reached Kilcullens' hill, you were straining your eyes to take-in everything, to miss nothing. What did you see, that first time you crossed the hill and looked down on Killeenduff? You remembered seeing Jack Conway sitting astride his horse-drawn mowing machine, Pat Conlon going the opposite way on his horse and cart, the two stopping for a chat as they drew level on the road. You saw James the

Jobber, sitting beside his white-washed gate-piers, his brother, Fat William, lurking behind him. You saw Willie Burns abroad in his field feeding a calf. You saw Jim Sheridan on his shiny new bike, his millionaire's hat perched sideways on his head. You saw Mary Conlon in her pinafore, crossing the road, a cupful of sugar in her hand for Bridgie Maloney. And you saw the smoke blowing across the road from Anthony's garden, a sure sign that he was boiling pots of potatoes on the outside fire for the pigs and hens. That's what you imagine you saw from the top of Kilcullens' hill. That's what I still see in my mind's eye when I now imagine crossing that brow.

With what excitement you watched Father turn the key in the front door. How you held your breath as you entered to find the house exactly as you had left it, but smaller, much smaller than you remembered it.

When the furniture was brought in and set up by the dozens of neighbours and cousins that had converged on the Corner, you were free to go, and you went, in all directions, like rocks from a blast of gelignite, Mikey to his namesake's, Uncle Mike, who had a farm down the Wrack Road with cattle and sheep, a jennet, and a pony for drawing the trap. Eileen went to Bridgie Maloney's, daughter of Little John, now deceased as they would say in the paper. You went off to seek out Anthony, to give him a hand with the last of the pots so you could both chase across the fields, hunting rabbits, or borrow his brother's fishing rod to try for some mackerel off the rocks at Cuangearr.

Yes those holidays were enough to sustain you for the year, enough to ensure the hob-nailed boots were always lagging far behind.

30

"**I** have to get out of the Scholarship Class. I have to." I was talking to Paddy who was standing beside me as we lined up two abreast to march to the Chapel for choir practice. I couldn't sing, neither could Paddy, but that didn't matter to the Master. He insisted that everybody in his class be in the choir and sing at early Mass on Sunday as well as at Devotions the same evening. He brought his prayer book with him everywhere, even to choir practice, and always held it in a particular pose, upright in his right hand, resting just under his left shoulder, as if proclaiming to the world, see how pious I am with my prayer book close to my heart. And it was the most enormous hulk of a prayer book I had ever seen, almost rivalling the size of the altar missal.

I was surprised when Paddy answered me, as I was merely verbalising the problem that was weighing down my mind, day in, day out. "Well you can't just leave. Your folks wouldn't let you, unless you tell them what's going on. So why don't you get yourself thrown out?"

I looked at him as if he were a prophet who had just resolved the riddle of my life.

"How do I get thrown out? By not doing the work? By pretending I'm a total idiot?"

The Master turned, satisfied with the file, and led the way to the Chapel. I felt as if I were walking among the clouds, surrounded by the sheer light of divine wisdom. Life was full of possibility once more.

As we were goose-stepping around the corner, Paddy delivered his considered response. "No, he would just beat the shit out of you. And if that didn't work he would complain about you to your father or your mother, and they would make you do the work for him."

We had reached the Chapel door when he leaned towards my ear. "Think of something that will madden him enough to throw you out."

Once inside we had to fall into a tense hush. If a single whisper violated the formality of our presence, the Master would point sternly and painfully at the sanctuary lamp glowing above the altar.

Upstairs, the class took up the well-drilled formation on the tiered benches, girls to the front, boys to the rear. As I was in the tallest category I was in the back row, scarcely visible to the Master. I stared at the sanctuary lamp, watching it flicker, as I always did at choir practice. During performance I usually concentrated on the top of the congregation trying to identify people by the backs of their heads. But now I was concentrating on the only live thing in sight, and it was the sanctuary lamp that provided the inspiration.

This was the place to rile him. The Master always displayed irritation in the Chapel even at an involuntary cough. So, yes, this was the place to rile him.

When the slight shuffling of feet stopped he mentioned the name of a hymn, struck a note on the piano, and began to wave his conducting arms above his head. The choir rose into song.

I was like a crow astray in a flight of skylarks, and my strategy had always been to mouth the words, uttering only shaped silences. Now I thought of breaking my long silence, of adding my raucous roar to the nimble sweetness of the voices around me. However, even if the choir broke up in laughter, he would hardly regard it as a major crime.

As I was pondering, I had my hand stuck deep in my pocket and was feverishly turning over a rubber handball, which I kept for playing against the school wall at breaktime. I suddenly became conscious of the ball, and looked behind me. There was a sheer windowless wall perfect for handball. I glanced back at the Master. He was still waving his arms manically, his head thrown back so that the black hairs in his nostrils were all on show, occasionally turning the palms of his hands upwards as if trying to lift the voices to new heights.

Slowly I eased my head out of his line of vision, shrunk down behind the line of tall backs, and stepped down from the rostrum. I took out the handball and tossed it against the wall of the Chapel. Plonk, catch. Again. Plonk, catch. Then I increased the frequency of the throws, concentrating so that I would not miss a catch and lose the ball, waiting for the singing to be halted and the enquiry to begin.

But the singing continued. He probably couldn't hear the plonk of the ball above the sound of the combined voices. Or maybe he was so enraptured with the hymn he was oblivious to everything around him. The students on the back row must have heard, they must have been watching me out of the corners of their eyes, but no one turned, no one even faltered on a note.

I tossed the ball harder and higher. And I had to concentrate all the more to catch it on the re-bound. But there was not so much as a nervous quiver in the singing voices.

Then, when I was wondering if he would ever notice, I was suddenly sprawled on the floor, holding my head. I hadn't seen nor heard anything, but when I rolled over I was looking right up into his face. He was prancing and fuming, his nostrils dilated, like an angry colt, holding back his fury, reluctant to vent it in the house of God, unable to control it either. He was brandishing his enormous prayer-book. He had clocked me with his prayer book, and if I rose onto my feet he was ready to clock me again. So I lay there nursing my head.

Finally, the singing began to waver, became disjointed, then tailed off into a stunned silence.

"Up," he hissed, trying to keep his voice down. "Back to school. Wait for me at my desk."

Everyone knew the ominous significance of waiting at his desk. It was either a thrashing or a wire pulling. In my case there was no doubt what was in store, and as soon as I reached the bottom of the stairs I put my hands in my pockets to warm them. Warm hands didn't sting as much from a

122

caning as cold hands.

I was not long standing at his wooden desk when the class came trooping back. He had evidently cut short the choir practice. The students were all eying me with sympathy and curiosity.

When they were all settled, some sitting in the benches, the rest in a row all around the wall, as was usual since there were benches for only half the students, the Master moved to the top of the room until he was standing beside me. He didn't have to call for silence. Everyone was waiting, petrified. They were obviously terrified for me, but they were also terrified for themselves as there was every likelihood the Master would wreak his fury on everything that moved before the day was out.

He spoke almost through clenched teeth with a voice that quavered slightly, so intense was the force behind every slowly articulated syllable.

"I have never before witnessed the desecration of the House of God. And I intend never to witness it again. I have never until today encountered someone who would treat the Temple of the Lord as a common ball-alley. I never dreamt someone would display such contempt in the full view of the light shining before the tabernacle."

He turned to me. His white face was so tightly drawn he looked in danger of doing himself damage.

"You are a disgrace." He spat the words at me. "You are a disgrace to your family. You are a disgrace to this school, and to me. When I am finished with you, you will have more respect for the House of God." And he reached under his desk for the jockey's stick.

I put my right hand out, and he stood back to take a good swing. Then the strokes began to rain down methodically. I was counting. Six on each hand was the most we ever saw him administer. When he passed six I stopped counting. I was concentrating on holding my composure, knowing that whatever number of strokes fell on my right hand would be repeated on my left.

He finally stopped and laid the stick on top of the desk

123

where its steel tip and its metal top glowered at the class. I could see the terror in their faces as they looked at it, and as they glanced at me in awe that I had taken such punishment.

"Now you will stand in the corner for the rest of the week," he declared, out of breath from his exertions, "and maybe for next week as well, until I have the stomach to teach you again after defiling the House of the Lord. And as for the Scholarship Class, your shadow will never darken it again. Scholarship students in this school have always been models of good behaviour. But that is another tradition you have dragged into the muck, you little ruffian."

I proceeded to the corner, the Dunce's Corner as it was known, because to stand there was generally the privilege of those who couldn't solve arithmetic problems, or translate the Irish Reader.

My hands were numb. I knew the pain would return slowly and inexorably and would last all the longer for the ease I was experiencing now. In that respite between the punishment and the pain, I could try to enjoy my victory. I had achieved my aim. I was out of the Scholarship Class. No longer would I have to spend three days a week in a cold sweat dreading the extra class and the Wire Puller's manoeuvring to keep me back when the three girls were leaving. I was free of him at last.

However, as pain began to assert its territorial rights to everything below my wrists, I began to think of my return home, of what would happen when Mother and Father heard what I had done. The agony in my hands was nothing to the agony in my mind when I thought of their disappointment, their embarrassment at the disgrace I had brought on the family, their outrage especially when they heard I had desecrated the church. Above all I feared that they would never again look at me with approval.

31

People ask me at readings what inspired my poem, 'The Vision of John Devine'. It is easy, and yet difficult, to explain. I tell them I once knew a priest, a wonderful teacher called Father Tom, who could expound on any subject from the attributes of angels to the soil nutrients in cow dung. He wanted us to write a poem, a nice rhyming rhythmic poem suitable for a Christmas card, about God. And in his preamble he mentioned the visions of St John of the Cross and John the Divine. I recalled a John Devine of my own acquaintance, wondering what he would make of God. An image came into my mind of my own gods, drawn from memory of these fields, of a man, my father, Anthony's father, Mike Maloney, standing on a headland in the shadow of trees, barely visible in the twilight, looking over a field he has just planted. He stands there, almost invisible, the day's work done, looking over his planted field, and he is wondering. It was twenty years later when I wrote the poem.

32

Digging potatoes out of the cold earth was a miserable job. But I had no inclination to complain or feel sorry for myself. I was doing everything in my power to work myself back into favour with my parents. Now that the evenings had been swallowed up by the advancing darkness of winter, Saturdays provided the only opportunity of wrapping up the few remaining chores.

Mikey and I had been out in the Shan's field after an early breakfast. Father was to join us as soon as he had finished his half-day at work. I was digging vigorously trying to have as much done as possible before he arrived. The roots in the ground made it difficult to extricate the potatoes, but when they did come out the peaty soil fell away and left clean bright nuggets shining on the dark brown ridge.

Mikey had the easy job, picking the potatoes into a bucket and carrying them to the pit. Still he complained. His back was sore. He was bored. His hands were sore from carrying the bucket. But still I pushed on, urging him to a little more effort.

When the pit, as we called it, oddly because it was piled over ground not under ground, had reached a reasonably acceptable length, I relented.

"Why don't you go and check on the cow?"

He looked at me incredulously. "Can I?"

"Yeah, but don't be long. I'll have heaps of them dug by the time you get back."

"I'll have the heaps in the pit twice as fast as it takes you to dig them."

"Right, that's a challenge."

And he skipped off. The cow was his delight. He had been out of sorts since Mother stopped doing the milking. He had always accompanied her. When he took over, Father had to combine milking the cow with a dozen other chores, and so Mikey was left at home.

The silence when he left was sheer pleasure, as was the aloneness of standing in the empty field. I leaned on the spade and gazed at the sky over Sliabh Bawn. The only clouds were a few streaks of raked whiteness high up, where the perfect V of a flight of wild geese showed an equal detachment from the world. Had the wild geese been as imperturbable passing over Sligo? Had they looked down on the little cottages of Killeenduff, and continued their journey without demur? How could they? How could they have resisted the warm breast of Lough Easkey, or the spirit-shocking wilderness of the Ox Mountains? Soon they would be over Ballyclare. If they looked down and spied Hazel in her back garden putting rubbish into her bin, would they waver, and wheel, and descend from their lofty heaven to refresh themselves with a glimpse of greater beauty?

I watched the relentless progression of the wild geese until they faded in the distance, seeking the south and no doubt the consummation of their own ecstasy. Then I remembered my own predicament and began digging again. No matter what, I could not be found wanting once more. And it was easy to keep day-dreams at bay when I was rooting with a spade and reaching down with my hand to shake spuds from a withered bunch of stalks.

Mikey returned and started picking up the trail of potatoes I had left for him.

"You never go to see the cow," he said to me. "Do you not like the cow?"

"I like the cow. Of course I like the cow. But there are enough of you minding her. And I have to get on with other things, you know."

"Well why don't you come over and have a look at her now. It's lovely to watch her eating grass."

"I don't know. We have to get as much done as we can before Daddy comes. He won't be too pleased if he thinks we

127

were off watching the cow eating grass instead of doing the work."

"But we have a huge amount done, haven't we? If we get this ridge finished we could take a break, couldn't we?"

I looked at the ridge and at the substantial pit of potatoes we had to show for our morning's work. "Alright then, full steam until we get this ridge finished, and then we'll go off and watch Pruggy eating grass." And I lashed the spade into the Shan's contrary earth.

We didn't pause until we had finished the ridge, and then dropped spade and bucket. Mikey led the way across the fields to where the cow was grazing.

"What do you think of her?" he asked.

"Well, I have seen her before, you know."

"Yeah, but not for a long time. We're feeding her the table-waste with Indian meal every night. Daddy says that's better food than she got before. Do you think she has improved?"

"I do. Yes, I think she has definitely got fatter."

The cow was looking at us benignly as if interested in the verdict on her condition. She was black and white, a Friesian, a breed that was reputed to be best for milk. The reputation was well deserved, judging by the huge bucket-ful of milk she delivered morning and night. That was more than enough for our normal needs, so we let some go sour for butter, which we made in the dash churn. When the butter was skimmed off there was plenty of buttermilk left for making soda bread.

Mikey was stroking the cow's head. "You can't milk her, can you?"

"No".

He knew I couldn't so I expected him to gloat. Instead he said, "come on, I'll show you."

"We'd only waste the milk."

"It won't waste that much." He had already crouched down beside the cow's udder. "Look at the way I'm holding my hands. Look," he said, showing how he had his thumb and first finger curled around the teat, the other fingers hanging somewhat looser. "Now, you have to squeeze like this." And he gave a deft little pull with his hand to send a spray of milk on to the ground.

I crouched beside him and let him direct my fingers around the teat. But when I squeezed, nothing happened, not even a dribble.

"See, I'm no good at it. You have the knack." I got up. Mikey was beaming. There was something he could do that I couldn't, and I resolved never to learn to milk the cow so that it would remain that way.

"We'd better get back," I said. "If Daddy arrives and finds we are missing, I will be in the bad books again."

We hurried back across the fields to where the spade and the bucket were sprawled at leisure.

"Why did you go playing handball in the Chapel anyway, Robbie?" Mikey had warmed to me considerably since my fall from grace.

I looked at him to see if he had heard anything of the background, but no, his open face showed that no rumours had leaked from my class to his.

"I had reason alright. I'll tell you sometime, but not now. I can't talk about it now."

He was looking at me with a bewildered expression, and I was reluctant to break the bond that existed between us at that moment.

"If I started thinking about it now, my hands would start aching." And I put my hands under my armpits, mimicking pain, dancing around the potato ridge.

Mikey picked up a strip of potato stalk and came chasing me. "Put out your hands until I give you another ten. You got off far too lightly, you did."

When we finished our play-acting, we resumed digging and picking the potatoes. I said to Mikey, "I'm going to get a scholarship in spite of him, wait and see."

"But you're out of the Scholarship Class."

"Yes, but I'm entered for the exam, and I'm going to do it."

"What's the point of the class so, if you can do the exam anyway?"

"He does two extra subjects in the evening, on top of the five we do in school. The exam is in seven subjects, so I will have to get more marks in the five than others do in seven."

"Everyone says he has it in for you."

"He has. But that's what will keep me going. I learn everything inside out so that he can't catch me, and that riles him all the more."

"If you slip up, he'll murder you."

"I know. If I keep that in mind and keep going until Easter, I might stand a chance of winning a scholarship. And if I do, it'll be thanks to him in a roundabout sort of way. But don't tell anyone. I don't want him to suspect what I'm doing."

"Alright, I won't tell anyone. I'm hungry. I wonder what time it is."

Mikey was always hungry, always eating, but now that he mentioned it, I felt hungry too. It was hard to judge the time with any accuracy at that stage of the day because the sun was squatting in the same spot just over the blackthorn hedge, and very little else was happening.

We kept working in dogged silence until the hunger made it obvious that we were well into the afternoon, well past the time when Father should have arrived with our lunch. The pit of potatoes had grown impressively long.

"What do we do now?" asked Mikey. "He should be here by now."

"Go up to the Shan's, and ask what time it is. I'll keep digging."

Mikey headed off in the direction of the Shan's house. I was worried. It wasn't like Father to be late for a job like this. Could anything be wrong? Was he reluctant to come out because of his disgust with me?

"It's half-three," Mikey declared with indignation when he returned. "No wonder I'm starving."

"No wonder," I agreed. I was really anxious now. The hollow in my stomach was caused by more than the absence of food. Father was never late for anything. When he set a time for something he was absolute about it. We often joked

130

of how he became a prisoner of his own schedules, insisting on keeping the most trivial commitment even when it would have been more sensible or even more important to do something else. He said he would come straight out to us after he got home and had his lunch. That would have been two o'clock at the latest. And he had promised to bring us hot tea and sandwiches for our lunch.

"What will we do?" asked Mikey.

I knew he was hoping I would agree to abandon the job and head for home to see what the problem was. But I was terrified of making the wrong move and wading deeper into the morass of my parents' disapproval. How would Father react if he arrived late at the field to find the two of us had absconded?

"We'll wait for another while. If you're tired take a rest, and I'll keep digging."

"But we haven't had anything to eat since breakfast."

"I know. If we keep working for another while, and he still doesn't come, then no one can blame us for going home."

It was more than a little while when Father eventually appeared. Mikey spotted him the moment his head appeared over the hedge at the road. He parked his bike in the usual place and crossed the wall where there was a break in the hedge, then came walking towards us, no bag of food in his hand, a lively jaunt in his movement. He was smiling as he ran his eye over the pit of potatoes.

"Boys, you've done a great job and you must be starving. We'll cover up the pit and head home until you see your new sister."

"A new sister?" squealed Mikey. "You mean Mammy's had her baby."

"That's what I mean, and the baby is fine, and your mother is fine."

"Yahoo," shouted Mikey, as he galloped across the field in the direction of the road.

"Hold on. We have to cover the spuds first." Father went down to the small cock of hay we had cut and saved from the headland around the potatoes. He loosened the ropes and

131

took an armful of hay. Coming back to the potatoes he spread the hay out over the pit. "Another lock of hay, and we will have it secured against the frost." He was happy as a lamb, but still I noticed he avoided looking me straight in the eye, so I could not tell if I had been forgiven.

"Tell us about her, Daddy," said Mikey. "What is she like?"

"I think she takes after your mother. It's just as well. You wouldn't want a girl to look like me." And he laughed at his own joke.

"And what will we call her?" Mikey was excited beyond bounds.

"We'll have to decide that. They were suggesting Angela, because the Angelus was ringing as she was born."

"Eileen will be pleased it's a girl," I said.

"She's delighted. And she was a great help. Your mother went into labour shortly after the two of you left this morning. Eileen was very cool. She called Mrs. Power, and then went for the nurse. Between them all, the job went like clockwork, and when I arrived home I was told the baby was born."

Mikey and I had forgotten our hunger as we tidied the potatoes and spread the thick pad of hay over the pit. When it was well covered, Father took the spade, dug a few lumps of clay, and placed them on top of the hay.

"That will secure it for the moment," he said. "It's a fine pit of potatoes. You did great digging, and great picking. I wouldn't have done any better myself." And I felt the aftertaste of my disgrace was indeed beginning to dissipate.

132

33

ehind the house is the great stretch of Rafter's field. Many times Father planted potatoes there. Anthony's father, too, often rented ground in it to sow his crops, as he was a farmer without land. But when the field was in pasture it was the common playground. All the children of the townland, all cousins of course, congregated there. It was there you first encountered Anthony. He was a few months older, and to a child who has just learned to walk, a few months older is almost grown up.

And one of those times you arrived back in Killeenduff and went to seek him out, his mother said he was digging the potatoes for the dinner. When you followed the track of the newly dug drill you found him lying among the stalks with a little plastic microscope he had bought through the post from a company that advertised on the back of comics. He was intently scrutinising an insect he had caught. And he passed the microscope to you. In the sharing of a toy microscope you knew you were home.

34

I knew something was wrong when Mrs. Power came to the door of the school looking for me. A cold feeling ran through my veins, my stomach flopped, my mind was in panic.

"Robbie, there's a problem at home. The baby's not well. Your mother and father want you to collect Mikey, Frank, and Billy, and to go home straight away."

What was Father doing at home? It was Monday. He had called us for school that morning and then gone to work. Eileen was at home. She was staying to do the housework and to help Mother for the few days she was in bed. Why hadn't Eileen come with the message?

It took a few minutes for Mikey, Frank, and Billy to collect their bags and coats. When they came outside, they were full of questions.

I just shook my head. "We're wanted at home. That's all I know."

Mrs. Power had gone on ahead of us and was half-way up The Park, her head lowered. That did not augur well. When we rounded the corner, we saw her going into her own house, not into ours.

My stomach felt sick, my head felt sick, as I went in the front door. Father was sitting on the couch with his head in his hands, but looked up as soon as we went in.

"We have bad news," Father began. His eyes were red and it was obvious he had been crying. That frightened me. "The baby died."

"When? How?" I asked, all sickness suspended in shock. Mikey and Frank sat down at the table and began to sob convulsively.

"What happened?" I was screaming but probably without raising my voice.

"This morning," Father began, faltering, "after you'd all gone to school, your mother was having a snooze, and she thought the baby was having one too. When she woke and took her up to feed her, she was ...." He broke off, couldn't repeat the awful word.

I stood there stunned, didn't know what to say, didn't know what to do. Then I felt a heave in my stomach, and I ran for the toilet. But the door was locked, there was someone in there, so I ran out the back, and behind the shed I disgorged my stomach. Heave after heave continued, even though nothing was coming, and I wanted to vomit up my life's breath, to be dead like Angela.

When the heaving stopped I leaned against the shed wall. I looked around. There was no one watching me. The Park was smothered in the silence that enveloped the houses when the children were in school. Now it was eerie, this silence, as if the world had curled back into its shell at the horror of what had happened. She was just a lovely little smiling baby. How could she die? How could she be let die? She was only two days old. What kind of life was that?

I went inside again. First I went into Eileen's room. She was lying on the bed crying, her hands over her face. Around her were the little bits of toys and baby-clothes she had gathered there in anticipation of Angela sharing her room. I tried to say something, that I was sorry – but that would sound stupid – that everything would be alright – but that would be a lie – so the words stuck in my throat unuttered, and I stood there in silence watching her cry.

Then I went down to the door of the front bedroom, Mother's and Father's room, my bedroom, where for the previous two nights I had gone to sleep listening to the light rhythmic breathing coming from the pram, where I was half-woken each night by her cry for milk. The black knob on the door looked formidable, as if it would take all my strength to turn it, as if it would open the door to hell itself. But I turned it, and opened the door. Mother was sitting up in the bed, her head and back supported by pillows. The pram was pulled tight to the side of the bed. I stood inside the door. At first glance I could not see Angela in the pram.

"Come here, Robbie," Mother's voice didn't falter, and even though her eyes were red she was not crying. "Come here and see your sister."

I dragged my leaden feet across the lino until I stood over the pram. I looked in. Her little white face looked no different to when she had been sleeping. But there was no movement from her. I reached in with the back of my hand and touched her cheek gently. It was cold and set, as if she were turned to wax. Her eyelids were closed, as if she had shut them on the world. But what did she know about the world that would encourage her to bow out so fast?

"We must all be brave now," came Mother's steady voice. "Angela is gone to heaven. She will be an angel watching over us. Do you want to bring in Mikey and Frank to see her?"

I nodded and went out to the kitchen. They were all exactly as I had left them what seemed like a hundred years earlier.

"Come in and see the baby," I said to Mikey. "She looks just as if she's asleep."

Mikey didn't budge. I went up to Frank and took him by the hand. Tears were still rolling down his bewildered face, but he came with me. When we entered the front bedroom I felt him stiffen, but once he saw Mother and heard her voice, he relaxed. She lifted him when he climbed up beside her and she held him in a tight hug. Meanwhile Mikey entered slowly as if he were tagging along. I stood at the head of the pram gesturing him to come and look. Slowly he edged his way through the room and slowly raised his eyes until he was looking into the pram. He stood there, staring at the little face peeping from the white frills of the little pillow, and the white frills of the little cover, as if he were trying to make sense of it all.

Trying to make sense of it was something I was striving desperately to do myself as I now withdrew to the back garden. Leaning on my bicycle, which was propped against the back wall, and staring into space, the grisly suggestion rose from the morass of my brain that it was my fault, that it was God's punishment for having defiled His house, that it was I who had brought down this curse on our family. I did my best to keep that grisly thought at bay, but nevertheless I wished it was I who was dead instead of Angela.

After a while Mrs. Power came back. It was evident that she had been in helping all morning. The Powers lived next door. I could hear her filling the kettle and taking out the mugs. Then she sent Frank around to call us all for lunch. I didn't feel like eating. I didn't feel like looking across the table into the faces of my brothers, my sister, my father. But it would be worse to absent myself, so I dragged myself back to the kitchen and wilted into a chair.

Father was in his usual place at the top of the table, but instead of taking his food with his usual energy, he was just sitting there staring into his cup of tea. He had Cormac on his knee, jogging him up and down in an utterly detached way. Eileen, Mikey, Frank, Billy, and I, we were all avoiding each other's glances, as if we were suddenly strangers, thrown together against our wills.

Mrs. Power was mercifully silent while she was pouring tea, cutting bread, finding things to put on the table.

Then she broke the silence. "The little angel is gone straight to heaven, and she will be looking after you all for the rest of your lives."

The words almost knocked me to the floor. Angela had not been baptised. She couldn't go to heaven. She couldn't go to heaven. How many times had that been drilled into us in catechism classes, and yet it did not slip into my consciousness until now.

I looked at Father. He was still staring into his cup. I wondered if perhaps he or Mother had given her the emergency baptism which anyone could administer to a sick baby. But Angela hadn't been sick. I expected the worst. But I had to know.

"Angela wasn't baptised, was she?" I asked.

No one responded. Father didn't so much as lift his head. Eileen started crying again, convulsively. Mrs. Power went

137

over and put an arm around her.

"There, there," she said. "The baby is gone straight to heaven. Believe me. And she'll be waiting there for all of you to join her."

But she wouldn't be in heaven. It was the Church's solemn word against the well-intentioned soothing words of Mrs. Power. And she wouldn't be waiting for us. We could never be together with her again. She was lost. In Limbo, the very word was more frightening than Hell. In Hell she might have the consolation of being in the company of some that loved her. But Limbo, that dark place where none of us could now go, sounded loneliest of all. To save her from that fate, all it would have taken was for one of us to pour some water on her head and utter the few words of the ritual. We had failed her. And now she was lost for all eternity.

I couldn't drink my tea, nor force any bread into my mouth, so when a little time had elapsed I got up and went outside. I leaned against the gable of the house, staring at the churned muck beneath my feet where everyone made a short-cut between the corner of the house and the back gate. I felt I never could look up again, never look at the sky, never face the accusing gaze, or the judgemental finger, of Him who had singled us out for punishment. Was it my actions in the Chapel? Or had we been guilty of pride, with our crops, and our cow, and our few pounds saved in the Post Office book? Did He feel we needed to be reined in? If so, He had done it, and with callous cruelty.

"Robbie." The voice seemed to come out of nowhere, out of the morbid silence of The Park. And I recognised the voice even before I raised my eyes.

Hazel was standing on the lane, looking at me. I didn't react for a second, for several seconds perhaps, wondering if she were really there, as I hadn't heard her footsteps approach, wondering if my own mind or the all-seeing figure in the sky was devising more torture for me.

It was only when she was about to step off the lane and wade through the muck towards me that I quickly reacted. It was Hazel, of course. As a Protestant, she was allowed off

138

the class before lunch while the Catholics studied Religion. I hurried towards her.

"Robbie, I heard about the baby when I came home. It's awful. I'm sorry." There were tears rolling down her cheeks. She reached out her hand, as an adult would, and I shook it as an adult would. But, unlike an adult, I could think of nothing to say.

"Can I talk to Eileen?" she asked when I eventually let go the tender warmth of her hand.

"Yeah, come on in," I said, and led her around to the front door.

When Eileen saw her, she just gasped, "Oh, Hazel," and wrapped her arms around her.

I left them there and went out again, feeling utterly inadequate, feeling the skies should fall, or that I should be able to tear up the rocks, and the woods and the houses and trample the rubble into the lake in order to give full vent to my desolation.

Albert Walsh came cycling up the road, and waved when he saw me. As usual, he was looking impeccable in his working clothes. It was a strange time of day for him to be coming home. After the footing and collecting were over, Albert got work clamping, tidying the long stacks of turf and ensuring the tops were clad with flat sods to ward off the rain. He was not old enough to get his own cards, so he was employed on piece-rate and was paid through his father's cheque, as for footing.

"Why are you home so early?" I asked when he drew alongside, and put his foot on the kerb to support himself.

"I was let go. We were getting too much done, and they were afraid they mightn't have enough work to keep the full-time men occupied for the winter. So they sent the likes of me packing."

"What will you do?"

"I don't know. Maybe I'll head for England like everyone else. Then again, maybe I won't." And he laughed with a mischievous inflection on the last phrase. And I gave a little laugh too, hoping he wouldn't go.

"How are things yourself? You look a bit down in the dumps."

"The baby died."

Albert stared at me with his mouth open. "When?"

"This morning."

"That's awful. I'm sorry."

I nodded while he continued to stare at me. What kind of monster was I that I could conduct a normal conversation, as if nothing was wrong, while the ground beneath me seemed to be howling its indignation? How could I have laughed at his little joke?

"Can I go in and see her? Is she laid out?"

"Yeah," I said waving my head in the direction of the house.

Albert left his bicycle on the side of the road and followed me. In the kitchen Hazel was sitting on the couch beside Eileen with an arm around her. Father was still sitting at the kitchen table, with Cormac on his knee, like a man that had lost his way.

"Is it alright if Albert comes in to see the baby?" I asked Father.

"Of course it is. Hello Albert," said Father, getting up, setting Cormac on the floor, and leading the way into the bedroom.

When Albert saw the baby in the pram, he too started crying. "I'm sorry," he said to Father and Mother in a hushed voice.

"Thanks, Albert," they replied almost as one.

And then Albert retreated. I saw him back to his bike.

"When is the funeral?" he asked as he remounted.

"I don't know," was all I could tell him.

By then the children from school were coming up through the estate. It was evident from the way they were passing silently and looking curiously that they had heard the news or had suspected the worst.

Hazel came out our front door. "I have to go now," she said to me.

"Thanks for calling. That was really nice of you."

140

"It was nothing at all," she said.

But she was wrong there. Whatever it meant to Eileen to have her call, it meant a lot to me. In a vague way she was hope. She was the same as us and yet different. She was beautiful and yet she walked the same concrete footpaths as the rest of us.

People began to arrive, adults. First came Ted Power, on his bicycle, his lunch bag on the carrier. He had obviously heard the news and downed tools, something which I knew would cost him a half-day's pay. He was the quietest man I had ever encountered, and tiny in stature, so his nick-name in the estate was predictable – Teddy Bear.

The children drifted back to school in little clusters, hurrying past our house in silence, like lambs who had sensed the bare-toothed presence of a dog. After they had all scuttled back to the safe fold of the school yard, the women started coming towards our house, with sad faces and rosary beads twined around their nervous fingers. And Mrs. Power stayed in the kitchen making cups of tea for the people while they sat and shared our nightmare.

There was something in the presence and sympathetic warmth of people that did help, helped to keep us living on into the next minute, into the next hour, helped to keep us from thinking the darkest thoughts of all.

And the people kept coming. The navy pram was now in the middle of the kitchen, and the buzz of sympathetic conversation was punctuated with rounds of the Rosary, the sorrowful mysteries, while the most sorrowful mystery of all lay wrapped in white blankets inside the battered old pram.

Mrs. Nally, our shopkeeper, with whom Mother had struck a deep friendship, arrived with a whole ham sliced up, and cheese, and butter, and about ten loaves of bread. Father went down to the Eagle and came back with bottles of whiskey and port in the shopping bag. And the people who came shook their heads at the incomprehensibility of it all, and sipped the whiskey, or port, or tea, and ate the sandwiches, and left.

As we edged into the night, people stopped arriving and

those who had spent time with us began to leave. It was about the time when Father would normally be enquiring if we had finished our school exercises, when he would be drawing our attention to sleep by winding the clock and setting the alarm. But the alarm clock had frozen into motionless silence in the morning, time had become irrelevant, and in sleep lurked terrors we did not want to encounter.

This was not a normal wake. Everyone had left. We were alone, looking through the haze of tobacco smoke at the pram, not daring to meet each other's eyes. Then Ted Power returned. He had called in when he arrived home at lunchtime, but we hadn't seen him since. He was carrying a box and when he laid it on the kitchen floor, we saw that it was a little coffin.

"I would have painted it, but there wasn't enough time for it to dry," he said, speaking more words at the one time than I had ever heard him do before.

"Thanks, Ted," said Father. "You're very good to have made that."

The coffin was made of plywood. There were little decorative scrolls on the side and an elaborate Celtic cross on the lid. Ted's hobby was fret-work, making things out of light plywood, and he had obviously come home at lunch-time to set-to and make this. It was beautiful, but when we saw it, we all began to cry, knowing for what purpose it was there.

Ted left without another word. The silence he left behind was screaming to be broken. My limbs were enormous weights hanging from my body. What were we supposed to do now?

Mother was reclining on the couch, supported by pillows. She spoke, and her voice was calm.

"It's time for you all to say goodbye to Angela."

"But we don't have to say goodbye now, Mammy," Eileen exclaimed. "We'll have her for another couple of days, won't we?"

"I want you all to be brave for Angela," Mother said. "God has taken her from us. It is His will, and we must not question it. Since God took Angela, He will look after her, and she will look after us. Now, I want you to listen to this. God took Angela before she was baptised, so she can't have a funeral in the usual way. She can't be buried in the grave-yard. So your father has to take her out tonight and give her a private burial. But it doesn't matter where her body goes, her soul will be up there in whatever place God has made for her, and we must realise that and remember it."

Eileen was crying uncontrollably. Mikey and Frank had sunk into themselves, saying nothing.

"Robbie, I want you to go and help your father. You must be brave and strong. And remember that what has hap-pened is the will of God. It is not for us to question or to understand His ways."

She needn't have worried on the last score. I could make no sense of the snuffing out of a child's life after two days. I think Mother sensed that, sensed too perhaps that I fretted I had brought down this misfortune on Angela with my des-ecration of the Chapel.

Mother went to the pram and lifted Angela out as if she were still alive. She held her up against her shoulder, hug-ging her. Father took the mattress, pillow, blankets, and cover out of the pram and fixed them into the box.

"Who wants to give a last kiss to Angela?" said Mother, holding her down for Cormac to give her a kiss, then for Billy, and Frank.

When it came to Mikey's turn, he said, "Can I hold her?" And Mother put the little bundle into his arms.

Eileen took her next and held her so long it seemed as if she would never let go. But eventually she passed her to me. Her little forehead was so cold when I pressed it against my cheek I wanted to hold her forever to get some warmth back into her. But that could not be and I passed her back to Mother, who gave her a final hug and kiss and passed her to Father.

Father held her out from him in his strong hands. He did-n't hug or kiss her, just held her reverently from him the way a priest holds a ciborium packed with the Eucharist. He placed her in the box, stood looking reverently down at her, then put the lid on the box. Ted had even left four steel screws in the lid, and Father turned them home.

We were sitting looking at the little coffin, not daring to think or talk or question, when the sound of a car pulling up outside broke the silence. There were no cars in The Park, so I immediately sensed it was significant.

"That will be Pete Casey now," said Father quietly. He went to the front door and opened it.

Pete lived a short distance outside the town on his family's farm and worked for the Turf Company. Father always spoke well of him. A young single man, he was one of the few people who had a car and he operated a side-line as an un-licensed hackney driver. Generally it was groups of young people who hired him to drive them to dances.

Pete was solemn faced when he appeared through the door. He glanced around at all of us, glanced at the coffin, and said, "Sorry." He went up to Mother and shook her hand.

We were standing around, as if we were the lost souls, as if it was we who had found ourselves in Limbo, until Pete eventually shuffled and asked, "Are you ready to go now?"

Father was slow to answer. "Yes, Pete, We're ready. Robbie is coming with us."

Mother handed us our coats, and we put them on. Father bent down and picked up the coffin in his arms. I went ahead of him and opened back the door. Pete was first to the car and he opened the boot. Father placed the coffin in the boot and closed down the door. He then went around the back of the house and returned with the spade and shovel. I got into the back seat of the car and Father put in the spade and shovel beside me.

When Pete had the engine running, he turned to Father beside him and asked, "Where are we going, Joe?"

Again it took Father a long time to answer. "We have to find a maring," he said.

"What?"

"A maring, a boundary between two places. That's where we have to bury her."

144

"Well there's a boundary between the two counties and the two provinces running through the town."

"It would be perfect if it wasn't a river. I was thinking of bringing her back to the boundary of County Sligo, on top of the Curlews."

My heart leapt. What a beautiful place to bury Angela that would be, right at the place where we once stopped, with the view of Sligo on one side and the view out over the Midlands on the other.

Father continued, "Would you mind driving that far? It's just beyond Boyle?"

"I'll drive wherever you want to go. That's what I'm here for."

We moved off, down through the town, over the bridge, following the dark road to Strokestown, Elphin, Boyle, the road we had travelled before, always in daylight, in different circumstances. It began to rain, and all I could see of the countryside was the narrow road framed in the two semi-circles on the windscreen.

The villages and towns we passed through looked as forlorn as we felt, with their street lights illuminating nothing but rain. After Boyle we began the winding ascent of the Curlews, and my eyes were fixed on the road ahead waiting for the road sign welcoming travellers to Co. Sligo. It was a sight that in the past sent my heart soaring, but not now. Now it was to be the gravestone of my baby sister.

Pete halted the car on the side of the road right beside the sign. Slowly and reluctantly Father got out. Pete followed him. I extricated the spade and shovel, and left them propped against the car.

I joined the other two figures, barely discernible in the darkness. Father was walking slowly along the road, surveying the ground to left and right. We came to the other sign which read 'Welcome to Co. Roscommon'. There was a distance of almost a hundred yards between the two signs.

"Where's the maring?" asked Father. "I suppose it's half way between the two signs."

"I suppose so," replied Pete, and he sounded perplexed.

145

We turned and walked back roughly half-way, then stood again.

"I forgot to bring the flash lamp," said Father.

"Don't worry about that. If you pick the spot, I'll bring up the car and direct the lights on it."

Father essayed off the road and across the ditch. Again he stood stock still. I had never seen him so wracked with indecision before.

"It's like a swamp in here."

Neither of us replied.

"Aren't they a heartless outfit, making us bury a baby like the carcass of a dog?"

"Heartless is not the word I'd use," replied Pete with feeling. "Is there no better place to bury her?"

"At home there were special places, marings between townlands, or a bit of no-mans-land left at the centre of the cross-roads. But mostly it was the maring between land and sea people used. That was the most usual, the sandy bunkers at the very edge of the sea."

"Are we far from there now?" asked Pete.

"Too far," said Father. "We'd hardly get there by dawn, and this is a job that has to be done in the dead of night, as close to midnight as possible."

"Well, what do you want to do?"

"To tell you the truth, Pete, I don't know what to do. I thought this might be a suitable place, but I can't bring myself to bury the little creature in a swamp on the side of the road."

"Do you want to know what they do around Ballyclare?"

Father waded back to the road. "Yes, tell me."

"I didn't mention it because you seemed to know what you wanted to do. Besides it's something people don't talk about."

"I know. I understand," said Father. "It was the same at home. Only the men knew the burial places."

"Well, in Ballyclare they bury the babies in the corner of the Protestant graveyard."

"The Protestant graveyard?" Father sounded astonished.

146

"I helped a neighbour to bury a child about a year ago."

"The Protestant graveyard!"

"Apparently they have no problem with these babies being buried in their consecrated ground. They seem to be more civilised about it than our lot."

"They allow Catholic babies in their graveyard?"

"Well, the babies haven't been baptised so they're neither Catholic nor Protestant."

I thought of the cosy little cemetery in the grounds of the Protestant Church where Hazel and her family went on Sundays, and I felt like screaming at Father, 'Yes, that's where we should bury Angela'.

"I wonder if that would be alright."

"It's what people do around Ballyclare, and it seems sensible to me."

"Would we have to get permission?"

"I don't think so. I think it's all done on the q...t. Nobody asks for permission. Nobody gives permission. Nobody knows its happening. Everybody knows what's going on. You know the way. The Protestants are decent about it. They know the predicament people are in. So they leave that corner of the graveyard free and every so often a new little mound appears, but they ask no questions about it."

"What do you think we should do, Robbie?"

I was aghast at the question, because Father was being gored by his dilemma, and sounded as if he really did want to know what I thought, really did want my advice. It was as if, at this bleak moment on this bleak road, I had suddenly become an adult. I tried to compose myself in order to deliver my response as an adult would.

"I think it would be terrible to bury Angela here. I think it would be much better in the Protestant graveyard where we could go to visit her grave."

Father pondered this for a few moments, then replied, "Alright. The Protestant graveyard it will be then." And we turned back towards the car, walking a little lighter, three abreast, and I matched stride for sorrowful stride with the man to my left and the man to my right.

147

35

I have always been intrigued by the blindness of St Farnan. You know the story - that it was caused by his walking to Skreen in the morning to visit his friend, St Adamnan, thus facing the rising sun, and returning in the evening, thus facing the setting sun. But I always found it more than a little lame. Why would a hermit who had chosen to live in this sacred grove be commuting to Skreen every day? Anyway, the amount of sunlight we get in Tireragh, morning or evening, would be unlikely to damage anyone's retina. However, the fact that he was blinded by looking at the sun is fascinating. Was he leaning towards an ancient impulse to worship the rising sun? This is far more plausible.

Alternan, named or re-named after the saint, or the Kieve as we knew it, was always a place of religious worship. Do you remember how the people flocked there during the appointed season, from Garland Sunday, the last Sunday in July, to the Fifteenth of August, the Feast of the Assumption. On those days, and on any day in between, one could follow the rigorous stations, but had to do them at dawn and be finished as the sun was rising. The season corresponded to the Feast of Lunasa, so, were these same rites being performed thousands of years before Christianity usurped both places and rituals?

Many times you did those stations at dawn, preferring the interim days when nobody was around. But when you returned on those holidays for the last fortnight in August, you were in time only for the communal celebration on the last day of the season. And the images of Alternan remained in your mind along with so many more, for the rest of the year.

I visited it the other day. It seems to be visited rarely

now. People come for the Mass on the Fifteenth of August, but seldom does anyone do the stations. Nevertheless, the place is still the same, the river gushing over the waterfalls down to the pools etched into the rock, the cliff face with the ledges where the saint slept and prayed, the well where he washed his eyes. Indeed it is still the same as it was described by Mad Sweeney, who sang its praises when he visited it fifteen hundred years ago: Alternan of the green hazels. And the hazels are still there, still drooping down over the river.

The atmosphere of overwhelming beauty, of mystery, suggest a cathedral for the worship of nature, and I sense that it was here our ancestors paid their respects to the supernatural beings for at least seven thousand years.

36

I was trying to go to sleep, my hand resting on the timber box I kept at the side of the bed. In it were all my treasured possessions, picture postcards of Sligo, cuttings from newspapers, but mostly books, the Golden Treasury, also books I had scavenged from the storage cupboards of Mrs. Nally's shop. They were old school books her sons had used. Whenever I helped Mother with the messages, I would pretend to be searching in the cupboards for some item. She had all sorts of unwanted stuff cast aside there, and when I came upon a book I found interesting I would ask her for the loan of it. She would always give a glance through it wistfully as if some long lost love letter might be tucked into it. Then she would hand it to me, always with the same words, 'You can keep it, I'm sure you'll make more use of it than mine ever did.'

And I did make use of them, I read them all, the History books, the Geography books, but particularly the English books. Ever since we buried Angela in the corner of the Protestant graveyard, I was having difficulty going to sleep. So I would lift the lid of the box gently, to not wake Father or Mother, and take out one of the English books. I would stare endlessly at one of the illustrations, or read a favourite poem over and over until I could recite it to myself. These I could manage in the wisp of light coming from the street lamp through the gap I had contrived between the curtain and the wall. The fewer pages I had to turn, the better chance I had of not being detected by Father or Mother, who would immediately order me to go to sleep. And that was easier to say than to do.

But I was trying. I was lying on my stomach. If I lay on my back I was vexed by agitating thoughts. On my stomach peaceful thoughts came easier. My hand fondled the reassuring coolness of the timber box.

The box was from the hostel, the billets Father stayed in when he came to Ballyclare. It was located on the edge of the bog not far from the workshops. One evening when Father and I were returning late from the footing, we encountered Bill Murray, the caretaker. He was loitering outside, smoking his pipe and Father veered over to say hello.

They were standing there chatting like old friends, Father complimenting Bill on how well the hostel was looking, Bill lamenting that there was no one staying there anymore. I asked Father where exactly he slept, and before he could answer, Bill volunteered to show me. Father shrugged, in an indulgent way. It was one of those summer evenings when it seemed daylight was endless and the sun determined never to quench its torch. We had a good day's work done, and every reason to be satisfied with ourselves.

Bill led the way along the clear clean concrete footpath that dissected the tightly cropped lawn, to one of the rectangular huts. He opened the door and we went inside. The folded bunks were piled on top of one another at the far end. The lockers were lined up together against another wall. Beside us was a stack of wooden boxes. Bill pointed out where Father's bunk had been located, and where his locker had stood.

I enquired about the boxes. Each man had one under his bunk and kept his valuables locked inside. Bill turned to Father and asked if he remembered Big McCarthy and the stone. A Clareman, renowned for his size and strength, he took a flat sea stone out of his box every night and held it in his hand while he fell asleep. One morning he forgot to lock it away, and when some of the men returned in the evening they saw the stone peeping out from under McCarthy's pillow. They had a good laugh, and one of them said it should be possible to skim that stone all the way down to the bog. Another took it up, went to the door, and fired it with all his might. 'You're right', he said, and they all laughed again. But when Big McCarthy came back and noticed he had left

151

his box open he searched frantically for the stone. He noticed the other men sniggering and he went berserk. The men had to flee. When they ventured back, all the furniture had been smashed to bits and McCarthy had gone. He was never heard of again.

Father asked Bill what they were going to do with all the stacks of furniture. They were for sale. I quickly asked how much the boxes were. Half a crown. Father asked me if I wanted one. I certainly did. Bill got Father to sign for one and we took it away.

I thought of Big McCarthy holding his sea-stone, and regretted I hadn't brought one back from Sligo, from Cuangearr, a stone that had been polished smooth by the tide over thousands of years. It might help me to sleep.

I couldn't chance taking out a book until I heard the even rhythm of slumber coming from Father and Mother. The absolute silence probably meant they were still awake, still wrestling in their different ways with unspoken and unspeakable grief.

Eventually I heard a whisper and sharpened my ears.

"Are you thinking about tomorrow's vote?" asked Mother.

"I am," whispered Father in response.

"How do you think it will go?"

"I don't know. I'm damned if it's carried. I'm damned if it's not."

"You worry too much."

"How can I not worry? If the men vote yes, we will be downing tools by lunchtime. We will all be outside the gate, and there will be no wage packet at the end of the week. If they vote no, I'm going to be left precarious. I could be the one the management pick on to show their muscle. I could be told to report to Bangor Erris next week."

"Bangor Erris isn't the end of the world."

"You've never seen Bangor Erris."

"We can always go back to Killeenduff."

"No, we can never do that. Go back, I mean."

"We were happy there."

"We were poor there, and we would have been poorer if

we stayed. No, we have a chance here. And now that we have buried the child in the soil of this county, this is where we have to stay. We failed her when she died without baptism. We can't abandon the little of her that's left."

"We didn't fail her. Get that out of your head. It wasn't our fault. And it doesn't matter where she's buried, because it's her soul that counts. And I know where her soul is. It's right above us now looking down on us. I know that in my bones. I am as certain of it as I am of my own name."

"And what about the church? Doesn't it have its spake?"

"I'm as good a Catholic as the next, but I just know it's wrong on this one. Angela is with the angels, and if you go on strike tomorrow, she will be looking after us."

"God bless your faith. But if she is looking down she might be watching us starve."

"How would we starve? Haven't we our own spuds and vegetables, our own milk and butter? Isn't that more than most of them have?"

"I worry about them too, especially as they will be coming out to support me."

"They're not just coming out to support you. They'll be fighting to get the union recognised. How many times has Donal Fitzgerald told you that? They will be fighting for themselves. They will be just using your issue to force the Company to negotiate with them. And if they can achieve that, the conditions will be improved all round. There might be no more threats of Bangor Erris."

"I think they'll vote to down tools alright. The baggers are due to go out in a week's time, so they reckon this is the time to strike."

"Then so be it. We'll survive."

"We might be left outside."

"I doubt it. Don't they have to get the turf cut?"

"Yes, but how badly? They have enough turf in the clamps to keep the supply going for a full year."

"Put your faith in God, and in Angela who will be looking out for us."

"The plan I have is that if the strike drags on I'll sell the house in Killeen."

"Would you do that? You built it yourself, you and your brothers. Could you bring yourself to sell it?"

"It might be no harm to burn our bridges anyway. While the house is there, so is the temptation to go back. We have planted our flag in this county, and this is where the family has the best chance of getting on."

"Maybe, but we'll see. God is good, and whatever happens will be for the best."

I lay in my bed petrified. I could scarcely breathe. Very little had been spoken in our house in the weeks since Angela's death. The awareness of the looming strike added to the sense of doom. Mother, with her dogged determination, her defiant faith, was the only solid ground on which our feet found purchase in the giving shifting quagmire of those dark days. She had suffered most, and I often wondered whether she really found strength in her faith or whether she felt it necessary to put on the display of strength for us. We certainly needed it.

Father's suggestion that he might sell the house in Sligo knocked the bed from under me, though. I had assumed it would always be there, always ours, always awaiting our return. It was unthinkable that we would sell it. We were born, all of us except Angela, in that house. As Mother said, we were happy there. It was also the scene of the ecstatic pandemonium that was our holidays. How could he even think of selling it? If we needed the money to survive, he would have to. But there was more to it than that. Maybe it was that we were too happy there, too attached to the place. Father obviously felt that we would never put down roots in foreign soil while we were still drawing our sap from the soil of Killeenduff.

The prospect of the strike had been foremost in everyone's mind for weeks now. But as the fatal day drew closer, there was less and less discussion of it, until it finally became the topic of our silence. Everyone was terrified of this spectre. As it was, families barely subsisted from week to week. If a man was sick and missed work, then he had no pay-cheque at the end of the week, and the family had to get their groceries on credit. It might take months to clear such an account. So what would happen if the men were out for two or three weeks? If all the men were out, would the shops continue to give them food on credit? Would they be able to? And if the Company took a hard line would the families all be ordered out of the houses? It was these imponderables that eventually froze conversation.

37

Since I came back I have been searching for an explanation of that strange journey you made with Father to the top of the Curlews, looking for the maring between the two counties. People talk more freely now of what was hushed and painful then. Besides, the Church has since come clean and admitted that Limbo was a fraud, a stratagem for stampeding their flocks into baptising their children with frantic speed.

Yes, it was the custom for the father to take the corpse of the unbaptised infant and to bury it at midnight on a maring, a border between two townlands or two parishes. And, yes, the no-man's-land in the middle of a crossroads was also used. But the most frequent burial ground in places such as Tireragh was on the edge of the sea.

I pondered this long and hard until it was beating inside my brain, pondered it often into the early hours. And then a spark of insight struck. A point on a border is neither in one place nor the other. It is outside place. And midnight, the moment between the old day and the new day, is outside time. What if the burial was a ritual? As the infant would be damned to Limbo in the Christian world, was it being offered to the sidhe in the hope of a better afterlife? The cracks in time and place were used by the sidhe to sally forth from their underworld, why would they not be used to access it as well? And the most distinct border of all, between the land and the sea, between the two elements, must also have been seen as the most powerful maring of all, and so was the most frequently used.

I put my theory, that such burials belonged to an ancient ritual of offering these children to the sidhe, to Tom Connor who is well versed in the old ways of the whole barony. He had never heard such a suggestion, but then it was not something people would have been likely to admit, given the Church's attitude to pagan practices. However, he added, there might be something to it, as some people buried their unbaptised infants in the fort above.

I was astonished at his final remark. It proved my theory to me beyond doubt. At last I understood why Father embarked on that bizarre odyssey with Angela's body, even if he never did.

38

"Robbie, isn't it?" For a moment I couldn't accept the reality of the sight in front of me, and I stared at the man even though I had recognised him immediately. I had opened the front door in response to a knock, and there he was, standing on the doorstep, Willie Morahan.

"Is your father at home, Robbie?"

"He's not here, Mr. Morahan. Would you like to come in?"

I stepped aside and he walked past in his blue suit and tie and gleaming white shirt, leaving the opulent whiff of whiskey and cigarettes on the air behind him. It was a Sunday evening, so there was repose and order about the house, and I was not embarrassed by his unannounced arrival. I invited him to sit on the couch. There was no one else in the kitchen at the time. Under his arm was tucked a package, rolled and covered in brown paper, carried in the manner bank clerks carried the morning paper, or the bank manager an umbrella. When he placed it upright on the table I realised it was a bottle.

"Father and Mother are gone down the village," I explained, wondering how Father would react to this guest.

"I'm sure they won't be long," he replied. "I'll wait for them, if it's all right with you, Robbie."

I didn't know how long they might be. They had debated going out at all. It had been their custom to go down to Mrs. Nally's shop every Sunday night. Mother would pick up a few groceries and have a long leisurely chat with Mrs. Nally, as there were very few customers calling at that hour of a Sunday night. Father would drink a bottle of stout at the counter while the women were talking. He was always reluctant to go into bars, as he couldn't afford to get into drinking rounds. But on this Sunday night everything was changed. The strike had gone on all week, so there was no pay cheque on Thursday evening, and Father had maintained he couldn't afford the luxury of a bottle of stout. Mother maintained that Mrs. Nally would be hurt if we didn't accept her offer of getting all our usual groceries on credit, especially as she had declared emphatically she did not mind when the credit was cleared.

"Would you like a cup of tea, Mr. Morahan?"

"Tea, Robbie? I'm sure you make a good cup of tea, but I'm on something stronger. Would you be able to get me two glasses?" He unwrapped the bottle. It was Powers Whiskey.

I went out the back to get the glasses. It was the opportunity I was waiting for. I went in to Eileen who was lying on her bed reading a book, and asked her to leg it down to Mrs. Nally's shop and tell Father that Willie Morahan was waiting for him.

When I placed the two glasses on the table in front of him, he uncorked the bottle and poured a lavish amount into each glass. He lifted one glass in his hand, as if he were going to propose a toast, and shoved the other along the table.

"That is for your father," he said, indicating the glass on the table. I was relieved. For a moment I was afraid he was pouring it for me.

"I've been meaning to call on your father for a long time, a long time. But then time goes by so quick. I've been meaning to have a drink with him, not just a drink, a session. We have a lot to talk about your father and me."

He took a drink from his glass, and I realised he was already inebriated. It hadn't been obvious beneath his self-assured exterior.

"We go back a long way, your father and me, back to the old county."

I had never heard Father suggest that Willie Morahan had been a bosom friend, rather an acquaintance, someone he knew, and Father knew a lot of people. I wondered about the purpose of this visit, wondered whether he had black news about the strike, wondered whether he was seeking to entice father to concede and undermine the strike.

159

It would take some persuading to have the men return now without the full concession of their demands. They had taken the vote on Monday morning, and walked straight out the gate. Some had voted against the strike, but still they joined the picket outside. It was all new to most of them, and they were terrified of what might happen next. But what happened was not expected. The first lorry of the McHenry fleet arrived to take its load of turf to Dublin. When the driver saw the picket, he halted the lorry in front of the row of men. According to reports he was a small wiry man with a powerful Dublin accent. He stood chatting to the men, asking them why they were out, while other lorries of the fleet kept arriving and stopping behind his. Before long there was a line of lorries back for half-a-mile, most of them McHenry's, but other lorries too.

Then in front of the crowd of bemused lorry drivers and earnest strikers the little Dublin man jumped up on the bonnet of his lorry and made a rousing speech. He belonged to the same union and was not going to drive his lorry past this picket. Father said his speech was unrepeatable because it was laced with obscenities. He railed against the employers, and the bosses, and the supervisors, whom he classified as creeping jesuses. He urged the men to stand firm, that they would get their rights, and urged the other drivers to follow his example. He jumped into the cab, started the engine, and with his horn blaring he turned around the lorry and slowly led the way back the direction from which he had come. The other drivers followed his lead, blaring their horns, and the whole cavalcade moved off noisily to the cheers of the dancing strikers. 'We have them now,' shouted Donal Fitzgerald. 'We have them now. They won't move a sod of turf out of this bog. They can't use the reserves to leave us out.' And the picket became rock solid, the men marching over and back across the entrance so that even a bulldozer would not get past without running them over.

"They tell me you turned out to be a good little footer," said Morahan filling up his glass again.

160

"Not that good," I replied, surprised he was aware even that I had worked on the bog, although I was quite proud of my achievements.

"I heard you were good."

"I never did better than a half plot in the day. Lots of people could manage a full plot."

"Still a half plot is damned good for a young fellow. But then you're fond of the books, I believe. Reading books and footing turf don't mix too well." And he gave a little laugh to himself as he refilled his glass once more.

"Do you know, Robbie, I was a good scholar myself when I went to Bunowen school. Master Joyce was the teacher then. You wouldn't remember him. He's long dead. But he said I was the best scholar he ever put through his hands."

I knew this wasn't an idle boast. Father and Mother often mentioned that he had been brilliant at school, and they knew this, not from personal observation because he had attended a different school to either of them, but from public rumour and retelling of his achievements.

"I could have been anything. I could have been a doctor or a lawyer. I could easily have been an engineer, but then I can't imagine myself as an engineer, after all the run-ins I've had with that lot."

He laughed and filled his glass again. I was marvelling at his consumption of whiskey, but it was not without effect. There was a slight slur creeping into his precise articulation. And I had the sense that he was about to become maudlin.

"Money was all we lacked, Robbie, money. You should see where I came from, Bunowen. Where you came from, Killeenduff, is like Meath of the pastures compared to Bunowen. My mother had five rushy acres and the widow's pension. And the rushy acres wouldn't feed a nanny goat. You should see the little cabin of a cottage, Robbie."

"I've seen it," I replied.

And I had seen the actual cottage his mother lived in. When we were down on holidays Father and I took to our bicycles and toured the whole area. He pointed out all kinds of landmarks I wanted to see, including the Griddle Stone. Along the way we passed through Bunowen and he pointed out the cottage in which Willie Morahan's mother lived, and it was truly a forlorn spectacle. I wondered why he hadn't built her a new house with all the money he had earned.

"You've seen it," he repeated, and he seemed a little disappointed, as if he would have preferred talking about it as some kind of figure of the imagination. "There was no way I could have gone to college or to University. But it will be different for you, Robbie. Stick to the books, lad, and don't worry about improving on the half-plot."

"Maybe if I improve on the half plot I will have the money to go to college and University." I tried to be flippant in order to lighten the conversation. "Father and Mother should be soon home." But I knew by now that if they had wanted to see him they would have been here already. It was a while since I heard Eileen come in the back to her room.

"Your father and I go back a long way, Robbie. I always meant to call, to get him out for a good session. We'd have had lots to talk about. He was a great footballer. Did you know that?"

Father wasn't just a great footballer, he was legendary. The shoe-box full of medals in the bottom of the press proved he was great, but it was the exultant way the people of Tireragh recounted his exploits and the exploits of his brothers that conferred legendary status on him. And I lived in the shadow of his fame. I had to endure the look of disappointment on their faces when they heard that I was shaping up to be the world's worst footballer.

"I saw him playing when he was in his prime. County final after County final. My God, Robbie, you should have seen that man picking the ball out of the clouds and running through teams, with the toughest of tough men bouncing off him as if they were no more than gusts of wind."

Yes, he was maudlin now, and his head inclined to drop. If he had thought so much of Father, why hadn't he secured the proper rate for him? And I wondered what the reason

162

was for his belated visit.

"Your father was a hard man, Robbie. And I was a hard man too. It's a pity we never had a proper session, the two of us, never stood in a bar like two Sligomen talking about old times."

"Maybe sometime," I suggested.

"It's too late, Robbie, too late. This is the end of one hard man."

"What do you mean?" I asked, puzzled but also slightly alarmed he might be considering doing himself an injury.

"It's the end of a hard man. Tomorrow I'm for Holyhead."

My heart leaped. Had he been sacked? Was the strike over? And I knew what Holyhead meant. It was the phrase used by all the emigrants to England.

"Why are you for Holyhead, Mr. Morahan?"

"I'm not Mr. Morahan, any more, Robbie, so just call me plain Willie. I'm for Holyhead because I've packed it in. I'm finished. What you see now is the end of a hard man."

"Why did you pack it in?"

"Because they wanted to transfer me. They offered me a job down in Offaly, transport supervisor. What kind of a job is that? Eh? Sitting on my arse watching locos going up and down the track. Can you imagine me doing that? I opened this shagging bog for them. I got it drained. I got the baggers out on it. Men with shovels, that's all I had, Robbie, men with shovels. We opened this shagging bog, and look at it now. They were all sitting in their offices, looking out the window at me. Now they think I'm superfluous because they have more and more machines. The time will come, Robbie, when there will be no man working on the bog unless he's driving a machine. You have seen it, even in your time. Haven't you? You've seen the stripper running down along the trench, where before there was a team of men cleaning the top off the bog where the bagger was about to cut. You've seen that change yourself, Robbie. And the collector. Look at all the men it took to throw the turf into the conveyor belt of the collector. Hundreds. Next year there will be none. They have a machine coming that will gather the turf

163

straight from the footings without a man laying a hand on them. Eventually they will have a machine to do the footing as well. Wait and see."

"What about the strike? Is it over?"

"If they had given Joe his rate, I would have ended the strike for them. I was prepared to drive out one of the baggers myself, but the shaggers wanted to know if I would finish off the work the fitters had left undone before the bagger could move. You'd think they didn't want to get things moving, the way they're sitting on their arses. If they let me have my way I would go down the west and come back with a squad of men who would soon put the show on the road. But no. They thought it was time for a change, and that I was badly needed to supervise the locos up in Offaly."

"Do you think they will settle the strike?"

"I have no idea what the shaggers are thinking of doing, but while the weather stays bad like this, they're under no pressure. The baggers couldn't go out yet anyway. So they're laughing. They don't have to pay men to stand around waiting for the weather to clear. They're saving a fortune."

"What will you do now?"

"Don't worry, Robbie. I'll survive. Over in England they're building roads by the new time. And they're digging tunnels under the city of London. There's plenty of work, real work."

He looked at his gold wrist watch and poured the last of the bottle of whiskey into his glass.

"Robbie, I'll have to go now. I told a few of my drinking buddies I'd see them in the Hotel before closing time. A final farewell session. You know yourself. I'm sorry I missed Joe. Tell him I called, and ask him to drink my health when he comes back." He indicated the glass of whiskey on the table.

When he emptied his glass, he stood up, sprightly enough I thought after imbibing almost a complete bottle of whiskey. I stood up as well, relieved that he was going at last. He turned squarely to me.

"Robbie, one last favour. Will you ask Joe to put the best complexion he can on all of this when he goes back down the old country. You know what I mean."

And he made a grotesque attempt at a conspiratorial wink. I don't think I came to like him any better, but I was beginning to feel sorry for him, to feel that maybe he too was a victim in his own way.

When Father and Mother came back half an hour after, I was full of the news I had for them.

But Father was grim-faced, and he just said, "You did well to warn us, Robbie."

I pointed out the glass of whiskey Morahan had left for him, and Father took it to the range, opened the door, and flung the whiskey into the fire. The puff of a blaze was his toast to the health of the hard man.

39

It was during that last holiday trip to Sligo that you and Anthony visited the souvenir shop in Easkey. You were looking for postcards with pictures of the locality to take back. You had got an old box camera and were photographing scenes and people, but the photographs on the postcards were better. While you were browsing through the stock, Anthony was examining the souvenirs. He took up a little thatched cottage made of plaster, examined it, and said to the shop-keeper, 'That's not very good, I could do better than that myself.' The shopkeeper was amused. 'Do you think you could?' she asked. 'Definitely,' said Anthony.

She went into a back room and re-emerged with a large packet of plasticene. 'Now,' she said, 'let's see what you can do. Come back to me when you have a thatched cottage made.'

So Anthony took the plasticine, and you returned to Killeenduff. Maloneys' thatched cottage was across the road. Anthony started modelling, the house, the garden, the gate, and in no time he had created an ashtray with the gate for a cigarette holder.

The next day you were back in the shop, and the shop-keeper was admiring his thatched cottage ashtray. She told him to come back in a few days, and she might have something to show him. You gave her three curious days, and when you returned you were confronted by a display of twelve copies of his ashtray all in chalk-white plaster. It was your turn to marvel. 'Are you as good at painting?' asked the shopkeeper. 'Would you be able to paint each of these, and if we sell them I'll give you a cut?'

It was Anthony's first commission.

40

There was a corner on the concrete footpath, a junction between the path that led up to our one-storey houses and the one that ran in front of the terrace of two-storey houses. The paths were narrow and set into the open lawn. When I saw Hazel approaching I knew we would meet on this corner, I knew we would converge until we were in touching distance, I knew we would have to practically squeeze past each other, and my heart began dancing its wild caper, and my mind froze numb.

When she reached the corner, she did not try to squeeze past. I was about to step out on the grass to allow her pass. But she stopped. She was smiling at me.

"Have you heard the news?" she asked.

"What news?" I wondered what grotesque expression might be on my face.

"The strike is over. Has your father not heard?"

"He's on picket duty today. He hasn't come back yet. How did you hear?"

"One of the men called in on his way home to tell my father."

"Your father must be delighted. He will get proper treatment from now on. They all will."

"They will," said Hazel, and I felt that her affirmation had tapered into a significant silence.

"They will have to give him a regular job from now on, won't they?" I probed the silence into which she had retreated.

"I suppose so, but it doesn't matter any more. We are going to England."

"To England!" I gasped.

"We had been planning to go for some time, but Dad wanted to wait until the strike was settled. He felt he would

167

be letting down the men if he left while the strike was still on."

"Now that it's settled, he's going to leave!"

"Yes, it looks like it."

I was finding it difficult to comprehend the logic of waiting to win proper conditions for yourself, and when all was won, walking away. The eight-week strike had left every family in The Park penniless, far worse than penniless, and the Martins would have been no exception. If they had decided to go to England, why had they not gone earlier? George had been treated so badly, no one would have blamed him for leaving. How could he have endured the eight-week strike, purely on the basis of principle?

"It's a shame."

But truly as I was wrestling with his logic, I was contemplating the awful consequence of his removing Hazel from my world.

"Yes," she replied, and her voice had dropped to a whisper.

"But why?" I asked.

"Mum isn't happy here. She thinks we'll always be different here. In England we'll have a better chance of fitting in."

"And do you think you'll be happier in England?"

"I think Mum will, yeah. I think Dad will too, but then he could settle anywhere."

"What about you?"

"I don't know. I'll miss this place."

"This place?"

I looked at the corner on which we were standing, suddenly conscious that I was loitering there talking to Hazel Martin for what might have been an eternity.

She laughed, recognising the perplexed glance I had cast around me. "I mean The Park. Ballyclare. But this corner too. We have passed each other so many times on this corner."

I was astonished. I had never thought of her being aware of me as we passed, even though she always smiled and said hello. Yes, on this corner we had passed each other a thou-

168

sand times. And now I wondered if such meetings had aroused in her the same jumble of confused emotions as they had in me. It was not conceivable.

"Our ghosts will still be passing each other on this corner when we are both dead." She laughed, but there was a sadness in the glint of her eye.

I wanted to rage that I could not find consolation in the hope of our ghosts meeting, that I wanted her to stay, so that every time I walked down the path I could entertain the delicious possibility of meeting her on the corner, that I could no more anticipate life without her than I could anticipate life without the sun in the sky, without the birds in the trees, without the road to Sligo. But nothing would come out of my mouth, nothing of all the extraordinary things I wanted to say.

Probably because I was standing there red-faced, sweating, weighted like concrete, she began to fidget.

"I'm on my way up to Ann's house," she said.

"Ok."

I was still rooted to the ground, all my faculties switched off, paralysis absolute. She turned to go, and that prodded me to an involuntary spasm like the graceless flap of a dying fish.

"I'll go back and tell them at home about the strike."

I walked alongside her back the fifty yards length of the path until we reached the lane at the side of my house.

"They will be happy the strike is over." She broke the awkward silence as we prepared to part again.

"They will. Still I'll be sorry to see you leave for England."

"Thanks, Robbie."

And I thought I saw her blush slightly, and I thought there was something musical in the sound of my name falling from her lips. But still she turned to continue on to O'Donnell's house, and I knew I would never have the opportunity of talking to her like this again.

I must have announced the ending of the strike with the tone of an executioner, because Mother looked at me sharply, there was such a discrepancy between the message

169

and the delivery.

"Are you serious? How do you know?"

"Hazel Martin told me. One of the men called in to her father to let him know."

Eileen and Mikey began to dance about the kitchen. Mother sat down on the couch as if in shock, as if she had to think deeply so that this outcome would really come to pass.

We had survived. At least we supposed we had. With the help of Mrs. Nally who had given us our groceries on credit, we had survived. Others had helped us too. On the first Sunday evening of the strike Charlie Rhatigan had cycled up The Park. I had not gone out after Mass for the eggs, as had been my custom, because we did not have the ten shillings to pay for them. Charlie took a shopping bag off the tall handle-bars of the bike and knocked on the door. He came inside, but would not sit down. He was on his way to the pub, he said. Then he placed the shopping bag on the kitchen table.

"They're your eggs," he said, turning to me. "I don't care when I'm paid for them, but I'll take it very bad if you don't come and collect these every Sunday. And if I'm never paid it won't cause me to lose sleep. There will be eggs and money after us when we're dead and gone."

Jim the Shan paid us a visit too. It was a Saturday evening about three weeks into the strike. He too had a bag, a farmers' jute bag, on the back of his bike. When he brought it into the house he pulled out a large plump chicken, freshly killed, un-plucked but for a patch on the breast. Jim pointed to this bald patch.

"Don't worry about that," he said. "I had to scatter a few feathers around the yard so herself would think the fox got the chicken."

The following day was Sunday and we feasted like lords.

But apart from those episodes there was little relief from the grinding effort to survive. The rain, constant from the day the strike began, pervaded our spirits. We knew there would be no settlement while the bog remained a quagmire, and so we were permanently watching the grey sky, permanently gauging the rainfall, permanently praying for a break in the cloud bank at the butt of the wind. For six weeks there was no relenting by the elements as if they were on the management side, as if they too felt an obligation to ensure that the workers suffered the consequences of their revolt. After six weeks the rain stopped, and the centre of attention was the bog, and the focus of conversation was on how quickly it was drying out.

When Father arrived home it was hard to assess from his expression whether all had gone well. This absence from the forge left him with a fresh complexion, but the seriousness of our plight had ensured that the gloomy effect remained.

We all stood around him waiting for him to speak.

"We're going back in the morning."

"Did they give in?" asked Mother.

"They did. They called in the shop stewards today, and said they wanted to settle."

"Just like that."

"Just like that. The bog is nearly ready for the baggers, so they have lost nothing. They have saved themselves a fortune in wages."

"Are they giving you your rate?"

"They are. And they were prepared to put George on a full-time rate as well."

"And that was that! After all this time!"

"Well not quite. The Union lads put the boot in, and handed them a list of twenty more grievances. They said they wanted regular meetings with the Management to sort out many other problems. That shook them, but they agreed to full recognition of the Union and weekly meetings with the shop stewards."

"That sounds great."

"It is. There will be no more bullying and threatening. It was a good piece of work, even if we did suffer for it."

We sat in to the table for dinner. Mother put the pot of bruitin in the centre and began ladling it out. It was our favourite among the economy meals that had sustained us over the eight weeks, the mashed potato with onion, milk,

171

and butter mixed through it.

"We will all be on overtime to get the baggers out," said Father, his mood lifting a little as he tucked into the bruitin. "And we will be paid at the rate of time-and-a-half."

"That sounds good."

"You could take it easy and get back the money you lost through the overtime so," I ventured to join the conversation.

"I don't think so. The men are as anxious as anyone to get the baggers out. The sooner they go out the sooner there will be turf for footing, and that is where they all hope to recoup. At this stage they would carry the baggers out on their backs if they had to."

"They're all under pressure," agreed Mother. "I don't know how some of them have managed to survive."

Father looked at Mother and then around at the rest of us. I sensed immediately that he was about to say something significant, something he had been nursing until this moment.

"I have a good offer on the house in Killeenduff, so I'm thinking of letting it go."

There was absolute silence. I was too shocked to speak. I looked at Mother. She was engrossed in eating her dinner, so I knew she had already been consulted.

"But why?" I eventually managed to speak. "The strike is over. You have the higher rate. When the footing starts we can earn enough to clear our debts."

"We have a lot of debts, and I don't like leaving people without their money. Besides, you will be starting secondary school in the autumn. There will be fees, and books to be paid for."

I wanted to say that I might get the scholarship, but that was a topic I could not mention since the time I was expelled from the class, even though I felt I had done well in the examination, very well in fact.

"The Maloneys are interested in buying it," said Mother in a subdued voice. "It would be nice to think of them living in it."

"But they have a house."

"It's in very bad shape. The day of the thatch is gone," said Father. "It would be much easier for them to move across than to build a new house."

This was more than I could bear and I lapsed into silence. It was traumatic enough to suffer the possibility of losing our own house, but it was intolerable to think of Maloneys' own house being no more. It was a thatched cottage in the most traditional of styles, cosy and dark inside with the front door always open. Father referred to it as Little John's but it was the family of the said John who lived there now, Mike and Charley, Bridgie and Katie, the warmest most hospitable people anyone could imagine. Located opposite our house on the Forge Corner, it was a rambling house for everyone, and everyone rambled. From morning until night people were dropping in to say hello or to exchange news. It was unthinkable that the heart of the townland would pulse no more. It was unthinkable that we would no longer have our own house to return to. And it was also unthinkable that Hazel was going to England and that I might never see her again.

41

Our ancestors on Father's side were stone masons. They built the chapel in Easkey, and when the parish ran out of money, they finished it on the promise of future payment. But when the priest had his church built, he ignored the debt, and they died in the Workhouse. You know that. You heard it a hundred times, didn't you? And you had it in mind when you attended Sunday Mass there. And you had it in mind when you looked up the enormous height at the choir singing for your First Communion and your Confirmation.

I have been back in the chapel for the first time. It was for Anthony's funeral. Anthony inherited the passion for stone. But he built no chapels. His creations were planted with love in the open landscapes in the full view of the heavens. I can imagine him enjoying eternal bliss only by looking down on the fields and the old whin bushes and the scattered boulders of Tireragh, occasionally casting a satisfied glance at his own creations.

42

I could feel the letter burning in my pocket as I made my way to school. Its message was burning in my mind, not in pain but in ecstasy.

It had arrived the day before. It was waiting for me when I got home from school, and my mother had propped it on the dresser without opening it. When I read the words, 'I am pleased to inform you that you have been awarded a scholarship....', my eyes lost focus, my hands trembled, my knees threatened to buckle. I stood staring at the tiny page until Mother took it from me and read it, then read it again aloud. There was laughing and cheering, perhaps even dancing, all around me in the kitchen, while I stood dazed and everyone passed the letter from one to another to read it again and again.

But by the time Father came home from work I had regained control of my wits. While he was in the full throes of joy and pride and excitement, I negotiated a concession from him, that I could leave school. All the other boys in my class had left as soon as the footing started, but of course Father had stuck to his principles. Not a day could I miss until the holidays came. Now I persuaded him that I had learned as much as I was going to learn, and that I would be better employed earning some money along with my mates.

However, I had no intention of leaving until I enjoyed the expression on the Wire Puller's face when he heard I had won the scholarship without his help.

The depletion of the class had seemed to discomfit the Wire Puller as much as it had discomfited me. He glowered occasionally at me across the empty desks but directed whatever teaching he still did at the group of girls. Mostly he assigned writing exercises while he mulled over the roll books.

This morning he called the roll, and continued totting up figures without assigning any work to us. After a few minutes one of the girls put up her hand.

"Yes, Mary, what is it?" he asked petulantly.

"I got the letter from the County Council yesterday, Sir. I didn't get the scholarship."

He was just a little ruffled. "That's too bad. What about the rest of you?"

The other two girls put up their hands.

"Sir, I didn't get one either."

"Nor me, Sir."

"That's a pity. But you have learned a lot by being in the Scholarship Class and gained valuable experience by sitting the examination. It will stand to you when you go on to Secondary School. You are all going on to Secondary School, aren't you?"

The three girls nodded their heads vigorously. He was about to put his head down into the roll books again when I put my hand up.

"Yes, Dowd, what is it?"

"I got a letter too, Sir. I won a scholarship."

There was a gasp in the room, followed by a babble of amazed whispering. For a moment I thought they were going to give me a hand-clap.

The Wire Puller looked at me and his upper lip curled almost to the tip of his nose.

"Didn't you do well, Dowd?"

"Yes, Sir," I chirped.

"I suppose you'll be off to Mel's, now that you've got a scholarship."

"No, Sir, St. Mary's."

"I suppose they wouldn't have you in Mel's."

"I don't know, Sir. I didn't apply."

He was getting redder in the face, and it was obvious he wasn't' going to win this exchange. It was obvious that the listening students knew he was being sarcastic and that I was being insolent.

176

"Well, God knows, St. Mary's isn't much of a place, but it will be good enough for you."

"Thank you, Sir. I'm hoping to do well."

At that he withdrew into his sullen silence. He was unsettled. He knew he had crossed a dangerous line by criticising the local school that most of the boys were going to. He could be in trouble. He could be embroiled in a serious row, and he knew it.

St. Mary's was the school that was opening on the Connaught side of the river. Rumour had it that it was being set up in a hurry by the Bishop of Elphin to pre-empt the opening of a Vocational School on the Leinster side. It certainly had the appearance of being planned in great haste, as it consisted of three rooms attached to the new parish hall. Paddy and Val were going there as well, so I was looking forward to it. Only those who thought they had a vocation for the priesthood or who had the money for the boarding fees went to St. Mel's in Longford town. We regarded it as posh, and no one from The Park even thought of going there.

43

Why did I never come back until now? It is a question I have been asked many times, a question I have asked myself many times.

I have never had an answer, not an answer you would understand anyway. Certainly, I was terrified of coming back, terrified that anything would have changed, terrified that the picture in my mind would no longer correspond to a reality, terrified that if I laid eyes on the new reality the power would be switched off on the images in my mind.

For seven thousand years our ancestors built and farmed, loved and married, were born and died on this stretch of ground between the Ox Mountains and the sea. Is it any wonder my pulse beat faster every time I thought of the majestic sweep of Aughris Head, every time I imagined Ben Bulben and Knocknarea stretching across the bay, every time I recalled the thorn bush on the side of the road under which Grandfather used to meet Grandmother when they were courting? Is it any wonder that every image of Tireragh haunted me until I wove it into words?

Sligo was my first love. And, like everyone's first love, it became the measure against which all subsequent loves were gauged. When I began to discover beauty elsewhere, there was a sense of infidelity, an uneasy feeling of betrayal. Even though I continued to serenade my first love with everlasting passion, the world was insinuating itself between us, and the distance between us kept growing. The longer and the more intensely I continued singing the more remote my beloved became, until eventually I knew I was serenading something that now existed only in my mind.

So I never came back. Yes, I was most terrified of what I desired most.

44

Beneath the bridge, at the base of its first arch, the big arch over the deep channel where boats plied and where we swam, there was an abutment, a little island of cut stone, an apron spread around the base of the arch to protect it from the gush and the rush of the swollen river in winter presumably. In summer it was the perfect base for diving into mid stream, and it was an adventure even to get on to it, as the only access was by climbing down from the parapet of the bridge.

It was a favourite stand for fishing. When you didn't have a fancy nylon rod with a casting reel to spin your bait half way across the river, then the abutment was the perfect stand. You could drop in your line tied from the end of a hazel rod, the gross hook scarcely hidden by a splayed worm, lead weights chewed securely just above it, a cork from a porter bottle as a float. Then you could sit on the abutment and watch the cork bob about in the middle of the river for hours on end.

In late September a continuous spell of warm weather set in that had played truant all the long weeks of the summer holidays. No doubt it was sent to taunt us, the sun rising in a golden haze as we cycled to school in the mornings, setting in a golden haze while we bent over the great tomes of Algebra, and Geometry, and Latin, and Science, strange new subjects with strange-sounding names. But we had a full hour for lunch and as soon as the bell rang we stuffed our sandwiches into our pockets, hopped on our bikes, retrieved our fishing rods from the hedge where we had concealed them and headed for the bridge.

There must have been twenty of us lounging all over the abutment, occasionally rising to keep our lines apart. There were fish in the water. We could see their shapes gliding past, great big fish, bream, or roach, or rudd. So we watched our corks with expectation while we ate our sandwiches. But whatever the fish were looking for, it wasn't our worms. And so the conversation rose.

"That was some swim of Art's."

"Jesus, yeah. What was he trying to do? Swim the length of the lake? Swim to Athlone?"

"It was a good job they found him on the island. He could have died of starvation."

"Not likely. Sure if Art swam from here to Saints' Island, he could surely swim from the island to the shore. It's not a tenth of the distance."

"Maybe he wanted a turn as Huckleberry Finn."

"Maybe he wanted to show what a good swimmer he was after coming back early from that Training Course."

"At least there were no wire pullers on Saints' Island."

"What do you mean?"

"After he came back from the course, he said to me, 'the wire pullers are everywhere'."

"Jesus, is that why he came back early?"

"He said to me that the kids were all a shower of bastards, that they weren't interested in swimming and improving at all, that they did their best to put you off so you wouldn't swim well and they would win."

"Yeah, he got needled all the time because he was from the country. Most of them were from Dublin."

"A pity. Art was good. He could have gone to the Olympics."

"Jesus, if the coaches were wire pullers and the kids were all little bastards, you couldn't blame Art for packing it in."

"Dead right. After all he went through. He had enough of wire pullers."

"What do you mean?" This question from one of the boys who hadn't gone to our primary school.

"Our old teacher, the Wire Puller - he picked on Art that time after his mother died, pretended that Art needed special attention. He used to bring him back to his own house in the evenings, to give him help with his lessons. You can imagine the help he gave him. Art's father was drunk all the time, and when Art told him he didn't want any more extra lessons, his father beat the shit out of him and told him the Master was so good to him he should show his appreciation."

"Where is he now?"

"Gone back to live with his grandmother in Erris. He's getting a job with a mechanic out there."

I did not participate in this discussion. I was thinking of Art alright, and that last conversation I had with him the night before he returned to Erris. He told me he had set out to drown himself, to keep swimming until he was exhausted and went under.

He swam as far as the Gut, a mile or more with the current, but that didn't tire him. Then he went through the narrow channel of the Gut and out into the open lake. He swam for another mile or so and began to feel tired. He let himself sink into the lake, down into the peaty brown depths, with the amber daylight thinning above him. But just as his breath was about to burst he shot to the surface like a buoy released to float. He swam another while, then tried again. Down into the depths of the lake he went, but just as he opened his mouth to suck in a soul-full of water he felt this push back to the surface.

Again and again he tried. But each time the lake spat him back. Art in his slow way of talking and serious demeanour described the sheer dark of the lake and the rush of amber light towards him as he shot to the surface. Every time he cleared his eyes, the lake and the sky and the distant fields looked more and more beautiful. Eventually this island rose before him, a lovely wooded island with ruins of old churches on it. There was no depth to the water now, so he waded ashore.

"Oh, huh!" Someone had looked up at the parapet and sort of grunted to draw our attention. Looking over at us was the face of Father Henry, his reddish blonde hair radiant in the sunlight, his habitually benign features hardened into a steely expression.

Someone who had a watch checked the time. "Oh, Christ!"

There was a silent fluster as lines were quickly pulled in and wrapped around the rough-hewn rods. There was a rapid clamber up the face of the bridge from plinth to plinth. As each one passed the stern-faced priest, he nodded, "Sorry, Father."

The priest's car followed the platoon out the road to the school. The fishing rods were incongruously propped against the wall beside the bicycles. Father Tom was sitting in his teacher's chair at the top of the empty classroom. He continued reading while we all traipsed in.

When the last of us was seated and the door closed, he raised his eyes and surveyed us.

"Boys, you have missed twenty two minutes of our English Class. We would have been studying Shakespeare's 'Merchant of Venice', one of the great masterpieces of literature. We were about to be introduced to Shylock, Shylock, that sad man, dehumanised and demonised in the context of the drama, and in the minds of all the generations of readers down to our own time. But perhaps you had more important matters to attend to. So tell me now, while I try to keep my annoyance in check, what important business came between you and the study of the 'Merchant of Venice'?"

There was absolute silence for a moment. Then one of the boys at the front who were heating under the intensity of his glare half whispered, "We were down at the bridge, Father."

"Down at the bridge." He paused as if to chew on this piece of information. "Down at the bridge. I have noticed since I came to Ballyclare that the bridge is popular within a certain element of the community. It strikes me, from observation, that it is men of no occupation who congregate on the bridge. I see them there looking around them, scratching themselves, smoking a cigarette. But I never see them doing anything useful or productive there. But I may be wrong, I may be completely wrong. You boys may have gained immensely more experience by spending twenty-two minutes on the bridge than you would have gained from our English class. You may have gained more profound insights into life by contemplating the river than you would have studying the character of Shylock. I should not be so facile as to assume that twenty-two minutes studying the Shannon was not more beneficial to you than twenty-two minutes in the classroom. So I will give you a reasonable opportunity to show me you have benefited from your sojourn on the bridge. In any event I am much too agitated now to teach you for the rest of the period. So open a blank page of your English copybook and write down an account of what you learned while contemplating the river. You have fifteen minutes to convince me that your time was spent more productively, and if you succeed we will forget the whole episode. But if you do not so convince me, then we will return to the study of the 'Merchant of Venice' on Saturday afternoon. Is that fair enough?"

The intense silence wasn't broken while we opened up our copies, but the absolute consternation was like a bolt of electricity. Detention on Saturday afternoon was unthinkable. Many of the boys were from farming families and Saturday afternoon with good weather in late September after a broken summer was priceless time, time needed for saving crops, digging potatoes, bringing home turf. Their fathers would be incandescent with rage if they were not available. Those of us from The Park had chores too and some were still getting a little piece-work on Saturdays from the Turf Company, tidying the clamps. Our fathers would be equally enraged.

The Wire Puller would have punished our misdemeanour by leaving our hands raw with strikes from his jockey's steel-capped cane. At that moment I'm sure a sigh of nostalgia for his direct method might have been detected from the rows of bent heads.

I wrote my heading, 'The River'. Then as I stared at the word, a vision of the river came alive in my mind. It was not the idle expanse of water that we observed from the bridge, but the river as Art had experienced it, the benign god that

183

had declined the sacrifice of its favourite son. It was the river that caressed him, that parted for him, those evenings he shafted through it, up and down, up and down, while we stood on the bank with the stop-watch marking his time. It was the river in whose brown depths below the reach of the amber sunlight lay mystery, the mystery of Celt and Viking, the mystery of scholar and craftsman.

I was still writing when Father Tom called halt. When I looked up I was conscious of everyone being finished already, waiting for me. But when I glanced at the faces and glanced at some of the copybooks in front of my classmates I realised that the river had not flowed for them, that it had frozen in the blast of their panic.

Father Tom flicked through the pile of copybooks like an experienced card-player dealing out hands. One after the other he dispatched them into two bundles, but when he was finished all of the copybooks bar one were in the same stack.

"As I suspected," he said, "most of you learned nothing from the time you spent at the bridge. I'm not sure how much you would have learned in class, but you would have learned something. Therefore we must compensate for the time wasted when we meet on Saturday afternoon. There is one boy who seems to have got something from his observation of the river, and that is you, Robert. I'm very impressed. It is a wonderful description of the river, quite poetic, if I may say so. In fact it gives me an idea, Robert. I'm sure you would be well capable of writing a poem about the Shannon and Lough Ree. I have been asked to edit a page of the diocesan newspaper, 'The Angelus' and I'm calling it 'Poet's Corner'. Wouldn't it be marvellous to have a poem about Ballyclare, and written by one of our own? If you come back on Saturday afternoon as well, I will give you samples of poems in praise of rivers and lakes. There is nothing to it, just a matter of applying yourself. What do you say?"

"Okay, Father."

There was resignation in my voice and there was tittering about the classroom, not spiteful, amused tittering at the irony of the outcome. Like everyone else I had a leaden feeling in my stomach about the Saturday afternoon. It was lightened a little by the complimentary remarks. And it was lightened a little more by my sharing the fate of my classmates.

I knew Father Tom wrote poems, not so much poems as verses for Christmas Cards and the like. He told us about them practically every day for the three weeks we had been in front of him. He would start an English lesson by reading out a poem he had written the night before about Baby Jesus in the manger. The rhyming was always precise and the rhythm as regular as a heart-beat. There was never anything new in any of the poems. The only exciting aspect was the enthusiasm with which Father Tom spoke about them. He was absolutely passionate about his mission to arrest the deluge of secular cards flooding in from China, with nothing but pictures of Christmas trees, and balloons, and Santa Claus. He had teamed up with an artist who was inspired by the great Spanish painter, Murillo, and between them they produced the genuine article, printed and produced in Ireland.

I went up to him at the end of the class and asked him if I could have a go at writing a poem about Sligo instead. I would find it easier, I suggested, and besides, 'The Angelus' was based in Sligo, the capital of the diocese. I was thinking of all the attempts at poems about Sligo I had in the box under my bed.

But he wouldn't hear of it. He wanted a poem about Ballyclare, and nothing else would do. Sligo was beautiful, yes, but so was the Shannon, the lake, the islands, the woods sloping down to the water's edge. God didn't limit his beauty to one county, I should understand, and besides there was nothing to it. Anyone could write a poem about anything, so why not employ poetry in praise of God's creation wherever we found it.

God didn't excite me as much as he excited Father Tom. My feeling for theology might have been knocked out of my head that time the Wire Puller coshed me with his gigantic prayer book. But the challenge excited me, and I still had this surge of feeling I had managed to pour into the essay.

He pointed out the notes on the structure of poems at the beginning of our poetry textbook, and told me to study them. Writing a poem he said, was like filling a cup. The notes in the textbook would give me the range of cups to choose from. What I filled it with had to come from myself. The cup could be very simple, like a ballad, and one should certainly start with a simple structure. It could also of course be very elaborate like a sonnet, but a poet would manage to write a sonnet only after years of practice.

When I told Father and Mother what had transpired there was no recrimination about missing the Saturday afternoon. Father suggested that, if the good weather continued, it would be no sin to work a few hours on the Sunday afternoon instead. The potatoes were still in the ground. I could go out and dig the week's supply for the family dinners.

Each night, after I had finished my homework, I turned to the notes on "Prosody", as they were called. I tapped my foot on the floor like a traditional fiddler to measure the beat in the lines, and whispered the rhyming words to myself. As Father Tom said, there was nothing to it. Then I was tempted by pride and had a look at the sonnet. Apart from the intricate rhyming it didn't seem more intimidating than the other forms.

A sonnet would really impress him, and a sonnet it had to be. I worked on it into the early hours every night. I wanted to have something substantial for the Saturday afternoon. I wanted to have it finished, if possible, so that I would get away early enough to dig the potatoes and save my Sunday afternoon.

When scheduled classes finished on Saturday we ate our sandwiches quickly and then piled into Father Tom's room. The sooner we got underway, the sooner we would be finished. I opened my bag, took out the sheet on which I had written my final draft of the poem, and placed it on the desk in front of the priest. I entertained the hope that he would

186

accept it and dismiss me straight away.

He took it up immediately and began to read it while the shuffling eased into silence. It took him so long he must have read it three times. Then he looked up at us through the top of his bi-focal lenses.

"Boys, this is extraordinary. Robert has written a sonnet, a perfect sonnet about the Shannon and Lough Ree. Now, I'm going to go straight home and type it. With a bit of luck I'll catch the printer and have it in my first column in next week's edition of the paper. Now what were you here for? Oh, yes, to learn about the Merchant of Venice. Well, there's nothing I can teach you that you can't teach yourselves by reading the play. So go home and read the play. And if you don't understand it, read it again, and again until you do understand it. Once you have learned to read, you don't need teachers any more. Now off you go."

None of us moved. We didn't believe we were free until he himself packed up and left the room. Then there was an exhalation of breath, a muted yahoo, a chorus of 'Good man, Robbie', 'Well done, Robbie', as everyone charged for the door.

It was two weeks later. My poem had appeared in "The Angelus." I was the toast of my class. Every night after I finished my homework I was having a go at another poem. And the poems were adding together in a small notebook.

Father lumbered into the room when he returned from work, as was his custom, to say hello, to look at me with all those cryptic text-books arrayed in front of me.

This time he had something in his hand which he placed in front of me on the table. I looked at it and began to unfold it. It was a page of the 'Irish Press' newspaper, crumpled, but pressed flat again, with little grease marks on it here and there.

"Barney Kelly had that wrapped around his lunch," said Father. That explained the butter-marks. "He was sitting beside me, and was looking over the bit of newspaper. The next thing he shouts, 'Jesus, Joe, isn't that your young fellow?' " Father pointed to an article on the page, headed

'Poets get a hearing in the Diocese of Elphin', and written by someone called Patrick Lagan. I could scarcely focus my eyes. The whole column was about Father Tom's new 'Poets' Corner', and there was my poem word for word in the national newspaper.

It was a while before I had gained the composure to read what Patrick Lagan had written. In the mean time, of course, the rest of the family were swarming all over me trying to get a look at it too. He said, 'I'd like to quote all these Elphin poets but space does not allow me. But since I've a particular fancy for the green land around Ballyclare, for its lakes, canals and above all for the spreading, majestic Shannon let me quote a sonnet by Robert Dowd of Ballyclare. He calls it: 'Lakeside Reverie.' Then followed my poem. And Patrick Lagan ended up: 'Every man, said George Moore – thinking of his beloved Lough Carra – has a lake in his heart. There's a poet who would agree with him.'

I was a poet. Patrick Lagan and the Irish Press said so.

45

The old public houses are no more. There are none left that I have discovered. The men in wellingtons slowly imbibing their 'mediums' of porter - do you remember? An old man under a tweed cap, leans on the counter, reflecting on life: 'Thank God we lived so long and did so little harm.' All are gone now. It would be easy for us to be cynical of that old man's pride, wouldn't it, we who have changed the face of the earth in our generation? What would be his assessment? Have we done more harm than good? Did we have the right to change everything, to replace the giants with windmills? Or did we renege on a sacred responsibility to preserve the earth as we received it, to pass it on, undamaged, in all its richness and diversity, to the next generation? You smile, the smile of the innocent. Of course you cannot share in the blame or in the achievement, encased as you have been in vault within vault.

There is no place for home spun wisdom in this shining lounge, no place for 'mediums' of porter, or men in wellingtons. A business couple sit down across the way, order chicken curry and lasagne. All's changed certainly. I wait for the arts officer. I'm ahead of time, as always nowadays. Am I finally getting like Father, impatient for the future?

I recall the first curry powder that reached Tireragh. Anthony's sister sent it back from somewhere, Hong Kong, I think. Do you remember? His mother laced it into the stew, as instructed, and invited everyone who happened by to taste it. The approval rate was nil, the response negative, it would never catch on, and as you children spat out the burning meat, you lamented the destruction of a rich stew.

The arts officer arrives, young woman with bright enthusiastic eyes. She is orchestrating a major arts initiative on the theme, 'Unravelling Developments'. She is inviting me, now that I have come back, to write a novel as part of this project.

'How can developments be unravelled?' I ask her.

'How can things stay the same?' she retorts.

She's right. Life sees to that. Death sees to that.

'You can tell us how it was, so that we can understand how it is.'

'Like Oisin, come back to tell all?'

'There must be so much you can remember.'

'Memories are like the fragments an archaeologist uncovers. That's how I feel now, like an archaeologist poring over the fragments of my own past.'

'And if you join the fragments together?'

'Unfortunately, I don't get the past. All I get is a story.'

She laughs. And I reflect that maybe there are two pasts, one external one internal. Even as we sift through the debris in the physical world, the relics of what was, we can also journey inwards into the recesses of the mind and soul, where nothing has changed. The bog has been known to preserve a man for a thousand years. Is there something of a bog in the psyche wrapping itself around everything, everyone, encasing them, preserving them intact?

'Maybe within us we each carry the child we once were,' I suggest. 'Wouldn't it be interesting to make contact, and hear his or her story?'

'What interesting story would your inner child tell?'

'What it was like to leave, to have to grow up and grow away from this place.'

'That would make an interesting novel alright. And do you think he would provide a greater insight into the past?'

'I don't know. How can I judge? I would have to be alive then and now simultaneously.'

She laughs again, and I add, 'Yes, he would certainly have a story to tell. And, after all, isn't fiction the only truth?'

190